THOT CHRONICLES 3:

Isis' Final Reign

Thot Chronicles 3:
Isis' Final Reign

KeanaMonique
Pontiac Mi 48341

ISBN: 9781087946641

Cover illustration: https://www.ieshabree.com
Editing Services: Eloquent Editing Services
Eloquentxperience@gmail.com

In Honor of

My God Mother

Thressa Lynn Mahone

Loving you and missing you more
September 1, 1953 – February 5, 2017

&

My Bonus Son

Christopher Darron Smith

Forever always, my baeboy
January 14, 1997-May 17, 2021

Salutes

First and foremost, everything I do, I do for my children. Jayce Marquies, you're growing into a man right before my eyes. I'm so proud of you. Your infectious smile, your caring heart, and your willingness to be the best you can be makes it easy to love you with everything in me. You are the reason I breathe and go so hard. Kahamuu-n, you are truly one of a kind. Your personality is developing into greatness. You will always be Mommee's Muu. I'm doing my best to leave a legacy for both of you. Jayce & Kahamuu-n, it's nothing, but Aashuq (Divine Love) forever.

To my mother Phillis, affectionately known as *Philly Dee*, thank you for sticking around to see this come to fruition. You are the air I breathe. You are the reason I am who I am. I love you.

To my forever best friend, Emkhet, you are definitely a force to be reckoned with. Thank you for all the trials we've been through. They have helped me overcome things within myself that I didn't know needed to be dealt with. You've always been in my corner whether I was right or wrong. For that, I'm grateful and appreciative.

N'Chanted Nails' clients, I thank each and every one of you for pushing me to finish this book. The time we spend together is never enough. I love you and I can't wait to see you again.

To everyone who has read the first two books, and has been patiently awaiting the third one, I want to personally thank you. My Beta readers, who have always had time to read, provide feedback, and help me reach my full potential with this one.

To my Golden Girls: Ebony, Yauna, & Salamah, thank you for always being there when I needed you, and most importantly thank you for being my friend. There are so many people I want to personally thank, but I don't want to omit anyone. However, I will say each and every one of you gave me something unique whether it was a piece of you that you may have shared with me while needing the inspiration to write, or you could have said something hilariously funny that I had to stop to write it down, so I wouldn't forget it. You mean everything to me and for that, I want to say thank you.

Prologue

I can't believe how everything played out, especially at the wedding. Never did I actually want to be the person who stood up to disagree with the marriage of two people, but De'Angelo had it coming. I just hope Brandi knows it wasn't meant to hurt her. She just happen to get caught in the web of deceit that De'Angelo was spinning. She's a wonderful woman and she's going to land on her feet. Wherever Brandi is, I hope she knows her worth.

Just recalling a few incidents that have happened in the past, I guess everything happens for a reason, and for the life of me I still can't see why I am always a part of things that have nothing to do with me. Like grandma always said, "the universe will show you what you need to see." For that alone, I always keep my head up, eyes forward, and ears open.

Then, there's Kareem. He's my lifelong friend, lover, confidant, and whatever else category I need to place him in. Kareem definitely shows up and shows out. He keeps me balanced and focused on the main goal.

I swear life happens in the strangest ways. Being in the real estate world, you meet people from all walks of life. Some you take interest in and others you just let them do whatever it is meant for them to do. Right now, I've come to a fork in the road when it comes to my personal life and my work life. This season is personal. I have goals I need to attain and no matter what happens I have to be sure that my children, as well as myself, are secure beyond a shadow of a doubt. I've done things I'm not proud of. Some people have been on the short end of the stick and it was never intentional, but in life, you sometimes have more losses than you do wins. That all builds strength, character, and resilience to make you who you are.

With all that being said, let the chips fall where they may. When the smoke clears, I will be the last one standing, so consider this to be my final reign. I've got another level to reach but for now, I need to conquer and take everything that belongs to me before I walk away.

Chapter 1

Isis & Kareem

As we were leaving the wedding, it was pure mayhem and it was my fault entirely. Damn, I couldn't believe what I had just done. Nobody actually stands up and says anything during that moment where the officiant asks that famous question.

Well, I did. I think I actually feel bad about it. I feel almost as bad as when I ghosted Jaylen after our sexual encounter on Belle Isle, but only this time it's almost 5 times worst.

As I'm replaying the incident over in my head, trying to iron out my wrinkled thoughts, Kareem interrupts my thoughts, "You good, ma?"

"Oh yeah I'm straight", I half-ass say.

But deep down, I know it's not true.

"I just can't believe what I just did. I mean I never meant to hurt Brandy. She was just collateral damage, but that no good ass nigga, De'Angelo, had it coming."

"Well, if you know that, then why are you letting it take over your mental space? Didn't that nigga put a dagger in your heart? You know I raised you to be a bit tougher than what you're displaying and rightfully so. I know you're hurt, but we both know he had it coming.

In a weird attempt to make me feel better, Kareem softens his tone and says, "Hell, he was even messing with yo' secretary."

As I butted in with a slight tone of disgust, "You mean my *assistant* Ronnie?"

"Yeah, him too," and we both laughed.

It seemed to temporarily ease the tension.

"Thank you, babe, you are always in my corner, good, bad, ugly, or indifferent."

Taking a deep breath while looking me directly in my eyes, Kareem replied, "Well you know, I'll never leave you stranded or feeling neglected in any way. As long as there's breath in my body, you know I'm always gone be here for you."

Now that shit made my love below ooze a little bit. It's been over 20 years since we met, and he still makes my heart skip-a-beat. My butterflies still flutter, every time I hear Method Man and Mary J.'s, ghetto love anthem "You're All I Need". I think of him. He is literally my best friend. Life would be ever so amazing if we were official, but even then, would the vibe be the same? Who knows?

Making our way to the car, the sun was shining, it had a slight overcast, but for whatever reason the temperature felt amazing. Hoping to get my mind off the current state I was in, I turned to look at him and asked him what it was that he needed to talk to me about. All I know is what came out of Kareem's mouth totally caught me off guard, like I wasn't mentally prepared for this part of the conversation.

He grabbed my hand and exhaled but this time he seemed to relax his body and he said, "Remember when I was just in Vegas a few weeks back? Before you start jumping to conclusions, no I'm not fucking her and we haven't in quite some time. But, I needed her to hold my cheese 'cause I didn't want to have all that bread at your house with the boys there. Now, she just called me telling me that her house just got ran up in and that my stash was hit."

As I'm thinking to myself, I don't know if I should be suspicious about what he is telling me or should be freaking out? I mean his demeanor is too calm and I'm hesitant to ask more about what's going on. I mean, Kareem is always laid back, nonchalant. But every now and again when his feathers get ruffled, you see another side of him. That side is not so pretty, and considering we're talking about his money, he's too passive. Now, I'm uneasy. But, what the hell? I'm nosy, and I can't help but ask.

"Ok...so you're just cool, calm and collected about a stash that just got hit, or am I missing something?"

"Naw, you ain't missing nothing. I mean what can I do? I got a good idea of who did it based on how she was talking, and she think I'm stupid, but I know she set that little hit up. They didn't get shit but $1000.00," as he started laughing.

I turned and looked at him with a slightly confused facial expression, "Alright now, I'm really lost in the sauce. Can you stir it up a bit? So, I can make sense out of all this."

Kareem turned to me and fixed my hair, and looked at me as only he could. I swear I can feel his soul.

"Listen doo wap, I had a feeling she was trying to squeeze me for some blueberries, and I wasn't trying to hear that shit. I kept telling her I'll let her know. So, she started acting shady at times. She would have her little brother and his homies come by to chill and shit. They are already known for doing H.I.s."

Before he could finish, I had to get a quick tutorial in his lingo real quick. As I raise my freshly threaded eyebrows I say, "Ok before you proceed, I need a vocab lesson: What is a blueberry? And what are H.I.s?"

With a look of slight disbelief, and his head tilted to one side, he responded, "Little one, come on now, I raised you better than this. Keep up with the story. A blueberry is a blue strip, a $100.00-dollar bill and a H.I is a home invasion. I'll break it down in non-street terms as I'm telling the rest of the story."

We both laughed and he proceeded to talk.

"See, when people like her start pressing a money issue, you go fishing and by fishing, I mean you start to bait the hook. You leave it out, so you catch the fish. So, I gave her $10,000 or so she thought."

As he is speaking, I'm doing my damnedest to follow the flow.

He continues, "But what I did was took $1,000.00 and some dummy money to stuff the pile. By stuffing the pile, I mean, I only put one blueberry on each stack so each stack had a real bill on top of the dummy money."

With what Kareem just explained to me, everything is clear, and the street vocab lesson is complete.

"Oh, now that's good shit! I swear I learn shit from you every day. So, if and when, I ever ask for some money, I know not to ask for a fucking blueberry and to always check the bills 'cause you be on some fraudulent bullshit. Bam!

As he proceeded to playfully push my head, "Don't ever think I would play you like that. You know the combo to my safe. You know how I get down. Now, get yo' ass in the car, so we can roll.

Chapter 2

Family

Pulling up to the house, I just love how all the yards are newly manicured and the flowers are just blooming. Oddly, it appears that we've got a full house. I really hope that's not the case because I'm tired. I want to have my wine and kick back with my boys.

Before I could enter the house all the way, here comes Dino.

"Hey momma, you're a hashtag. You're a hashtag," as he playfully runs around.

Curiously, I look over to Ryan and say, "What is he talking about?"

With a devilish look, he asks, "Aye, momma, what did you do? He is right. Yeah, you are a hashtag, #weddingstopper".

I couldn't do anything but laugh. Instigating from the other room, Kareem is in the back getting his stuff together but talking heavy shit.

"Ryan, man, you should've seen her. She was definitely the show stopper. She was in rare form and the shit was funny. Believe it or not. But, I won't spoil it for her. I'll let her tell you. I'm about to go. I got some shit to go handle."

As I made my way back to the bedroom to have a few words with Kareem before he left, it seemed as if something was weighing heavy on his mind, I only assumed that by the way he was throwing his stuff in his bag.

"Are you ok?"

"Yeah, why do you ask?"

"You're throwing that shit in the bag like it did something to you. You know, damn well, when you're bothered everything about you is altered-from the way you look, your mannerisms, and the tone of your voice."

"Little one", as he started to laugh, "That's why I love you. You know me. You don't have to pry it out of me or nothing. Yeah, I'm a little bothered by the bullshit Mya trying to pull on me with that fake ass robbery."

With a look of sincerity I asked, "Do you think going over there tonight will be a good idea? I suggest, "Maybe you should just lay low tonight, in case something else in the pot is brewing. Hit it bright and early in the morning. You know. I'm just thinking. She told you about it, so you could come by there. What if she does have something to do with it? Then, maybe the 'supposed' robbers are waiting for you to come by tonight. Just stay here and leave in the morning that way you're not expected to show up. People won't have their guard up. There's more than one way to skin a cat."

He stopped doing what he was doing and just looked me right in my face. Then he grabbed me by my throat and threw his tongue down my throat so deep, I instantly got wet. As we're standing there in my room kissing passionately, he leaned over and pushed the door closed. He walked me over to the bed.

Still kissing me with so much intensity he began to whisper, "Let me have my way".

Before I could fight the feeling, he pushed me on the bed, lifted my dress, opened my legs and pulled my panties to the side. I just knew he was getting ready to fill up my palace with the joystick. But, instead, he gently kissed it.

With each kiss he slid his tongue up and down my clit. I can't understand why he has the look of a natural born killer, but in the bedroom he's just as sensual as they come. As he is enjoying the juice box, he gently inserted two of his fingers with just the right amount of force. He turned his fingers upward and did the come here motion while inside of me. Stimulating my G-spot, my body started to tingle. With every motion he did with his fingers, his tongue was doing tricks on its own. I didn't know whether to scream or squeeze his head with my legs. Nevertheless, he knows how to get me to the finish line.

He looked up at me with his face full of me, and winked his eye.

He said, "Are you going to give me my nectar?"

Referring to my love juice, I slowly nodded, "Yes."

I laid my head back and relaxed as he began to play and eat at the same time. I swear his tongue is amazing. I don't know which one to concentrate on, in order to release it.

At this point, I'm totally lost in the heat of passion. So, I just closed my eyes and let go. Before I knew it, my body began to shake and a quivering sensation came over me. Instead of allowing the sensation to control me, I decided to control it. I applied a little pressure as if I was releasing my bladder and all of a sudden it happened. I started to squirt. I can't even explain the feeling I was experiencing, but it was truly an out of body, euphoric experience.

I could hear him saying, "That's right baby, give it to me. Soak my flavor savor."

The more he talked the more I released. It just kept coming out and it wouldn't stop. Just when I thought it was all done, he took his left hand and applied pressure to my abdomen and told me to push. I did what I was told and gladly found I had more to be secreted. This time he opened his mouth to swallow every bit of his nectar as he called it. As he swallowed, he sucked and continued to do that until my well was completely empty.

Laying there on the bed, I need to shower and gather myself. I needed to go back and chill with my children, talk a little shit, and have a glass of wine. Kareem stood up and looked at his beard in the mirror, and all I seen was sparkles from the lights. I guess I soaked him up pretty good.

Laughing out loud, I said "So, your beard is drenched with my syrup? So that means you're staying here tonight, huh?

With no hesitation he replies, "Yeah". He replied while still looking in the mirror.

"I already made that determination when you broke it down to me about the expectancy of my arrival."

Next, he turns and looks at me while continuing his conversation, "I swear you are the female version of me and that's why I need to make it official between us. I'm gone wife you up."

Surprised to hear him actually say those words come out of his mouth.

I said, "Boy, stop playing! You know you are not ready for all that."

Kareem leans on the bed and begins to speak in a serious tone, "You know me well enough to know I don't say shit I don't mean. I didn't say I was gone do it right now, but it's coming in the near future." After he pauses, his tone changes from serious to playful. "Now, quit talking and go get yo' ass in the shower. So, we can go out there and kick it with the boys."

I swear his authoritative voice turns me on. As I'm gathering my bearings, I took a mental break to think about what just happened to my body. I remember reading in a book once about female ejaculation. It explained once she experiences this, her eyes will be opened, and she will be the Goddess she is destined to be. Well, I'll be damned; I guess he just opened my eyes to a new reality. So, now let's see what new shit I can see out of these jewels of mine.

Just as I am getting out of the shower, Ryan knocks on the door and asks me to come here.

Kareem throws me my robe, and I head out to see what's wrong. To my surprise, he wants to have company, again. So, I guess I'm not gonna get my peaceful and quiet night with my family. I look at Ryan and consider his request, just to mess with him. Just as his facial expression begins to change, I let him off the hook.

"Well sure why not? How many guests are you having over? How long will they be here? I know it's a Saturday, but I really just wanted to have a chill night with yall. For some reason I think you try to sabotage my time.. Do you think I'm too old to chill with?"

Laughing at my sad attempt to make him feel bad, Ryan says, "No Momma, you tripping. It's just the fellas with their girls and they won't be here long. I swear you won't even know they're here. Tomorrow I promise it's all us." Then he playfully says, "You are getting old, but never too old to hang out with."

Then he kissed me on my forehead and went about his way.

Before I could get back in my room, he yelled out and said, "I'll send Dino with two glasses and I'll be back with the drinks. Love you, Momma."

Damn, I love my boys, so I guess I'll go back to my room and get on Kareem's nerves as I retire for the evening.

KeanaMonique

Chapter 3

Isis & Avery

It's Sunday morning: a day of pure relaxation, no office work, no bullshit, no drama, I'm just going to sit around the house, and do absolutely nothing.

"Good morning, future wife,"Kareem said sleepily.

Covering my nose, I say to Kareem, "Ugh I see someone still has morning breath."

We both laughed.

"So what's on the agenda for today?" I asked.

"Well, I'm getting ready to go handle this business over at Mya's house after I get out of the shower. I got to go check on Dukes and Gammy. Then, I'll head to the studio. You know how my Sundays go. What about you?"

Smiling with a sideways grin, I say, "Absolutely nothing, I'm not doing any work. I'm just going to relax at home. I will probably fire up the grill and kick it with the boys. Hopefully, they won't want to invite anybody over. Hell, what time did those kids leave last night?"

With a look of confusion Kareem says, “Shit, I was knocked; All I remember is getting out of the shower, having a glass of wine, cuddling with you, and it was over.”

Leaning over to grab my phone off the nightstand, as I notice that it’s lit up, well how many missed calls and messages do I have? Oh wow!, 6 missed calls and 14 messages. What the hell happened between me going to bed last night and waking up in the morning? Before I could read the messages, my phone rang and it’s Avery.

With a perplexed look on my face, I answered, “Hey girl, what’s good with you?”

“Nothing. I called you to find out if it’s true about you being the hashtag weddingstopper?” She inquired.

As we both laughed, I had to admit that what she heard was true.

Smacking my lips, I told her, “Girl! That shit was so funny, but it wasn’t; if that makes sense. I needed to blast that nigga, De’Angelo, but I never wanted to hurt Brandi. But as they say, all is fair in love and war, right?”

“Hell yeah, no disrespect to Brandi, but shit she’ll recover. Women always do. As far as that nigga goes, he's fucked in the game–socially, professionally, and financially. Good job, Isis, my dear, good damn job."

Curiously I ask, "Well why say good job?"

"Simply because you've blasted him for trying to be a player and hell, Ronnie outed him for being on the down low. That's how you end a situation and bring closure to that.Now get up, so we can meet at the Caucus Club for lunch. So, I can give you this tea on Lance. He's at it again with another trollop. But, this girl is the nanny of the neighbor in the backyard. Girl, he's fraternizing with the help. Hurry up, Caucus Club 1 hour." Then, the call disconnected.

So much for relaxation, let me get my ass up, check on the boys and bust a move really quick. I swear I really just wanted to lay around all day. But, I guess it's gotta be some shit 'cause Avery never calls me this early. Besides, I need to get tighter with her anyway. Maybe she can help me get my own real estate company, since she does own Whitaker Construction. My grandma always taught me to build friendships with the most unsuspecting people. That way if some shit hits the fan, you always have an ace in the pocket, and today my ace in the pocket is Avery Whitaker. She's about to become my new BFF.

Pulling up to the Caucus Club, I hope I'm not under dressed. I wasn't sure how to dress, so I just put on my True Religion Jeans, a shirt with a cardigan, and some low boots. Hopefully, she ain't on no "beat a bitch ass tip" 'cause the universe knows I'm not in the mood, but I'm always with the shits. Entering into the building I see her already seated in a booth and she clearly looks like she hasn't had a good night's rest.

"Hey Avery, I'm scared to ask you how are you 'cause clearly you look like you need some sleep."

We laughed, and her response told me everything I needed to know. It seems as if we have some type of telepathic connection. That is weird. She looked at me with the face of a very vulnerable woman.

"Please have a seat. First off, thank you for coming, I honestly didn't know who I could call or at this point or who to trust. I know we haven't known each other for a long time, but I feel like you are someone I can confide in."

As she begins to pour her heart out, she says to me," Listen, I grew up with a house full of men, and I try to be the strong one all the time, but this shit that I'm going through with Lance is new for me. I try to be strong because that's my defense mechanism. But deep down, I'm hurting. Before I blow a gasket and have his ass come up missing, I need to let this out of my system."

I reached out to touch her hand to comfort her.

"Well, I wasn't expecting all that but whatever it is, please know that I have your back. It's not about the length of a friendship, but the strength of the friendship. So with that being said,. If you're hurt, I hurt. I'm here for you no matter what."

"Thank you so much. I really appreciate that," said Avery with a gentle smile and meek voice.

Now, she goes into detail about her marital problems.

"So, a short while after I found out about little Miss Kupenda and Lance, I came across some other interesting information. Apparently, he's been frolicking with another little trollop and I just happened to be outside on the patio. I saw his car on the street in the backyard at the neighbor's house. At the time I paid it no mind, I assumed he was meeting with her husband, but when I dug more into it, they had been separated for a few months. It's just the wife that lives there now."

Before I dive in and ask any questions, I made eye contact with the waitress, so I can get a drink, because this is clearly gonna get thick really quick.

"So, what makes you think it's the nanny?"

"Well because I had one of my postal workers keep a close eye out on who's at the house when they deliver, you know cars, activity, etc. Well, the worker said the children are always there and a young girl happens to be the babysitter. But, the mother is never there."

"Follow me real quick, I'm going somewhere," she laughed. "Now you know I know every time he swipes that card, and who goes to Air Time in the middle of the day? You know Aniya is in school or with Ryan, and his bad back behind ain't jumping on a trampoline. So, I had to put my workers on it. The information that came back to me was that her name is JahZanique or Nunuu as people like to call her. She's about 34, 2 kids, 2 different daddies, with a recent eviction, and she got the nerve to be babysitting for somebody else. I hope she doesn't think Lance is about to be her come up. She is going to find out that I'm the boss behind the money. As far as he goes, I swear his time is running out. I'm almost out of options when it comes to him. So right now, the only thing I can do is sit back and continue to collect my data until it's time to bust his head til the white meat shows."

We instantly started laughing.

"Girl, if you didn't just sound like Bernie Mac, rest his soul. But, I understand how you feel. I had to hold that information about De'Angelo when I found out that he got Brandi pregnant when we were engaged. Now, Avery, when I tell you I have your back, just know I do, and whatever you need me to do, consider it done. I'm getting ready to put my squad on this little Jahzy girl. By tomorrow or the next day, I'll have a full run down. No worries."

We sat there in an awkward silence for a moment or two.

Then all of a sudden she said, "I'm the daughter of a kingpin. He just doesn't know who I am or what I'm capable of. I'll cut his testicles off and use them as Chinese meditation balls." As she mimicked the twirling motion in her hand, she said, "I'm going to have to remind him of who's in charge here.. But first I'm going to juggle them like I'm in a circus."

The waitress returned to take our order and from there on out it was girl talk with the usual chitter chatter and laughing. We were just two women getting to know each other and starting what appears to be a great friendship

Chapter 4

Isis & Ronnie

It's Monday morning and I'm walking into the office. I don't know if it's me, but everyone seems to be staring at me as if they know what took place over the weekend. Hell, they probably are looking at me like I'm the bitch that ruined that wedding over the weekend. Well, keep looking. Yep, I did it. But enough of my outside persona, let me be professional, because I do love my job. I made sure I waved or winked to the people I locked eyes with, and of course I did it with a smile.

Ronnie comes in and says loudly,"Good morning #WeddingStopper, I mean you do deserve the hashtag."

"Ronnie please don't sit there and act like I did all that nonsense alone. I knew what I was doing. However, who knew that you had a few tricks up your sleeve as well?"

Twisting his neck, like only he can, he blurted out, "Now Boss Lady, you know I was NOT going to let his behavior slide with me, and to think I was really starting to like him."

As he looked down at the tennis bracelet that De'Angelo had given me that I gave to him.

"I understand and it truly is an unfortunate situation, but like my granny said a few times in my life, 'if it don't come out in the wash, it's coming out in the rinse.'"

"Wait a minute, that's a new one," Ronnie says, "Ok now, Granny got all these colloquialisms. It's hard for a little 'hood boy like me to keep up. Now, what does this saying actually mean?"

I explain, "Well in a nutshell it just means, you'll get the truth one way or the other."

"Alright Granny, well shut the noise. I might have to use that to let my goof troop think I know a little bit more than real estate and fashion," Ronnie said. He might as well have ended it with two snaps in a circle.

"Well Ronnie, that saying alone won't cut it but I get your point. Getting straight to business, we have a few things to do today. It'll be an in-house kind of day. We've got to create a social media flier for the website, and we need to go on Instagram and the other sites to spread the word about the open houses that are coming up. Also, contact Mrs. Melinda Jacobs about the pre-approval program. We need to also create an email blast for the company's website, so we can let everyone know about what's getting ready to take place."

I snapped my fingers in front of Ronnie's face, "Hello did you hear what I just said? Where are you? Hello, hello?"

Ronnie playfully snaps out his daydream and skillfully, word for word, repeated everything I mentioned.

"I swear sometimes I wonder about you. But when you do stuff like that, it amazes me. You and that memory of yours are why you're my favorite assistant."

"Correction Boss Lady, I'm your only assistant."

Giving each other that fist bump and a wink, as we head off to do some office work, I can already tell today is going to be a great day.

"Boss Lady, you have a call on line 4."

"Ronnie who calls on line 4? Wait! Was it a male or female?"

Ronnie responds and says, "It's a female, but she doesn't sound familiar but then again I don't keep track of all the people's voices that call. But, what we do know is to call on line 4 it's somebody that knows you or knows of you."

"Take a message, get a number, and I'll call her back."

"You got it." He yelled back.

A few moments later he walked into my office with a weird look on his face, and you could tell he wanted to burst out laughing, but he kept his professional attitude.

"Who was it and why do you look like you want to laugh?"

"Boss Lady, I thought Kupenda had a messed-up name. But, this lady that just called you, her name was Horisha."

I let out a slight giggle and said, "I'm bewildered as to why someone named Horisha is calling my phone. Who is she? What does she want with me?"

Shaking my head, I motion for Ronnie to sit back down.

"I'll call her back in a few but sit down, I need to pick your brain about a young chick you may or may not know."

"Boss Lady, now you know I got all the tea, so let me hear what you got. Then, I can get you what you need."

"Her name is JahZanique but her," before I could finish, he blurted out "NuNuu?"

"I mean I guess, but you didn't even let me finish."

"Boss Lady, there's only one JahZanique in the 'hood, and baby listen, let me tell you her and Kupenda do not get along. I repeat, they don't fuck with each other. Why do you want to know about her?"

Trying not to spill my beans too early, I just say to him, "Well, not to divulge too much information at the moment, but she may be in something that's way above her pay grade. But like I said, I can't say too much about it. I'll keep you posted and you keep me posted. But why don't she and Kupenda get along?"

"Whew, Chile it ain't enough hours in a day to tell you that story, but I'll sum it up by saying Kupenda shook the wrong tree and instead of getting falling leaves, she got NuNuu."

Now, this is getting interesting. I'm intrigued.

"Ok, now Kupenda was messing with NuNuu's man?" I asked.

"You can't call community property anyone's personal possession, but to make a long story short…YES!"

Shaking my head in amazement, I gotta put these pieces together quickly, so he doesn't get suspicious.

"Now, I thought Kupenda was messing with Mr. Whitaker. Are you telling me that the community property is Mr. Whitaker?"

"Boss Lady, this is gonna go quick, as he starts his explanation, "before Kupenda met Mr. Whitaker she was messing around with this lightweight baller named Jug and Jug has a baby by NuNuu. Once NuNuu found out about Kupenda, she quit messing with Jug. Since Jug wasn't a big weight mover, Kupenda found no real use for him and on top of the fact he didn't have a woman. That is just the beginning to the NuNuu vs. Kupenda saga, so NuNuu made it her business to make Kupenda's life miserable by terrorizing her from any angle possible."

"Yeah, that was a lot to digest. Thanks, I think I can follow the story correctly now. Do you have Horisha's number? So I can call her back."

He passed me a sticky note and went back to his desk.

Meanwhile, I'm sitting here at my desk thinking this all kind of makes sense. If Kupenda, messed with Jug, who happens to have a baby by NuNuu, and

NuNuu vowed to pay Kupenda back, then that's only right that she messes with Lance. Instead of an episode of *Girls Gone Wild*, it is like an episode of, *Hoes Gone Wrong*. Ok, I think I got it, but it is not enough to tell Avery. Now back to this Horisha chick, I honestly don't know who she is and what she wants with me. Furthermore, how did she get the number to line 4? But one thing for sure, I got her number and before I call her back, I'll check around and see if I can dig up a little info, so I can be prepared for whatever happens when I call her back.

"Ronnie, can you come here and bring a notepad with you please?"

As he was entering my office, the phone rang, and he paused mid step. "Should I go back and answer that or can I just pick it up from your desk?"

"No worries, have a seat, I'll get it this time."

Laughing, I answered the phone, Key's Real Estate, Isis speaking how may I assist you today?

"Bitch, I'm gone fuck yo' whole life up. I can't believe the shit you pulled at my wedding, you and that faggot ass assistant of yours."

"Listen you bum ass nigga, and listen to me very well. Don't you ever in yo' muthafuckin' life call my phone attempting to make fucking threats. I deal in money- back guarantees around this bitch. As far as you calling me a bitch, that shit don't phase me. Come with something better than calling me a bitch. Furthermore, keep Ronnie name out yo' faggot ass mouth. At least he owns his shit, that's something I can't say for you. Finally, you better be glad that's all I did at the wedding, and you lucky you still breathing around this muthafucka, 'cause, I could've had you buried my nigga. So the next time you wanna call my phone and be 'bout that life, remember my name is Isis Muthafuckin' Carrington, and ain't no hoe in me." And I hung up the phone.

"Ok!, Boss Lady, let me find out you around these streets carrying bodies."

Laughing hysterically, "Boy, stop, I ain't no killer, but don't push me."

"Boss that just solidified it for me, anybody going around quoting Pac, is definitely 'bout that life, and I didn't think you was old enough to know about him for real, so seriously, how old are you?"

"You tried it. You'll never find that out, and besides I'm old enough to be your mother. Now, let's get back to the matters at hand. Did you contact Mrs. Jacobs about the pre-approval program? And did you create the social media flier?"

"Yes, and yes. The proof is in your email awaiting your approval and Mrs. Jacobs said she's open, just give her your potential dates so she can lock you in."

"Well then, I guess that ends our day today. Thank you for a smooth work day and I'm looking forward to the rest of the week. We got some houses to sell."

As we were getting ready to leave the office for the day, he said to me, "Um, did you call that Horisha lady back?"

"Nope, not yet, I have to find out more about her before I call. I can't potentially be walking into an ambush, especially after De'Angelo called. For all I know those two are in cahoots together. Gotta be careful out here, you know."

"Alright boss, have a great rest of the day, and I'll see you tomorrow."

KeanaMonique

Chapter 5

Isis

Walking to my car, I'm actually stunned that this dude had the audacity to call my phone and try to play me with those weak ass threats. He clearly knows who I roll with, as a matter of fact, let me call Kareem right now and let him know what just took place.

"Pick up the phone Kareem. Hurry up and pick up."

As I'm summoning the universe for him to pick up the phone, my request was granted just before I hung up.

Sounding as if he's out of breath, he says, "Aye little one, what's good?"

"You'll never guess who called my office today. Nope, never mind, I don't have time for the shenanigans De'Angelo. He was talking cash shit, saying he gone fuck my life up. He called me a bitch and he even called Ronnie a faggot. I lit into his ass so tough. I told him I'm Isis Muthafuckin' Carrington and ain't no hoe in me, then I hung the fucking phone up."

As he took a deep breath, I knew what he was about to say was vital to my safety. He says "I knew this shit was gone happen. Listen, where are you?"

"Leaving the office, why?"

"Please tell me you got the piece in the car?"

"I do."

"Good, keep your eyes open, pay attention to everything and go straight home, I'll be there within the hour."

Then, our call was terminated. As I start to scratch my head, I'm really left in a state of bewilderment. But whatever, it'll make sense later.

Well damn, he didn't even let me tell him about the rest of my day. I better get my ass home and pay attention to my damn surroundings. I really needed to stop at the grocery store, but he did say go straight home. It is just one stop. Let me detour, so once I'm home, I don't have to leave again. I guess this small stop won't hurt.

Just as I was planning out my grocery list in my mind, my phone rang.

"Hello, this is Isis speaking."

Kareem's voice was full of sternness as he started to speak, "You really don't pay attention to the caller ID, but I got a feeling that you about to be on some bullshit. Take yo' ass straight home. I'm on borrowed time. I got moves to make and I don't have time for you to be lollygagging, I'll grab dinner. Take yo' ass straight home." Again, the call was terminated.

I screamed as loud as I could while I was in the car, "Why does he know me so well? And hell, if he knew I was going to be on some bullshit, then ain't no need to call him back and ask him what he is grabbing for dinner because he already knows what we eat. Damn you, Kareem.

While I'm in the mobile office, I guess I should make some phone calls. Who am I kidding? My children are already straight and Kareem is bringing dinner. Oh yeah, I need to call Avery. The least I can do is see if she has some more information on this new little situation. I just have to be careful not to let the cat out of the bag just yet. It's not that I'm not ready, it's just that I have to make sure what information I have is legit and factual before I share it with her.

It seems as if the phone didn't really get a chance to ring before she answered it.

"Hey, Avery, it's me Isis.

How's your day going?"

“Hey girl, it’s going alright just running Aniya around for the prom. We are making hair, nail, and waxing appointments. You name it, we're out here doing it.”

As we laughed together in unison, “Well, in that case, I won’t bother you with all the other stuff that we went over yesterday, so when you have a moment call me so we can talk.”

“Girl, please, Niya knows how shady her father is and I don’t hold anything from her. I need her to see firsthand how niggas are, so she don’t get caught up in no bullshit.”

“Well, I don’t have any solid information as of yet, but I will say I’ve got some strong sources on it. So, within the next few days, I’ll have more information. I just wanted you to know I was on it.”

“Oh girl, trust me, that’s one thing I don’t have to worry about with you. You are a woman of your word. I know if you say you’re going to do something that I don’t question it. I know it’ll get done. But, thanks for letting me know.”

“For sure. Well, I just pulled up at the house, so I’ll speak with you soon.”

Finally, I made it to my house, and to my surprise, I beat Kareem. But, I couldn’t help but to notice a few cars sitting in the cul-de-sac. One is in the entrance way and one in the dead-end part. That is suspicious, especially for this area. It's definitely something to pay close attention to.

Entering my house, all I hear is Dino playing the video game being interactive with the people in cyberworld.

Then, Ryan says, "Aye! What's up, Ma? How was your day?"

"Ryan, it was cool. Thanks for asking. There was a bit of drama, but nothing I can't handle."

Laughing he says, "Yeah, ok if it was something you could've handled then Kareem wouldn't be on his way over here."

With my hands on my hips I inquire, "Um, excuse me? Just because Kareem is on his way doesn't mean I couldn't handle my lightweight, and besides you already know I can't even break a nail without him tripping. So gone somewhere with that damsel in distress malarkey."

We both started laughing, he started to catch me up with details about Dino, prom stuff and college applications.

"Speaking of college,you still need to submit the applications but don't be alarmed when you might have to take online courses with all this COVID-19 stuff going around? It's bad enough that y'all might not even have a prom, and if y'all do y'all gotta practice social distancing and wear masks. While we're on that topic, what about graduation? They are doing drive-by birthday parties, and baby showers. Hell, who knows how your graduation is going to go?"

"It doesn't matter if I don't walk across the stage, getting my diploma is the most important thing. I know I don't have to worry with you being my mother. I know you may have something up your sleeve."

I couldn't do anything but hug him and cry on the inside because I raised a great man. If I can help it, the streets won't get either of them. Standing in the kitchen having a moment, in walks Kareem with dinner. Just as I suspected, my favorite, he went to the Mediterranean place and got the food. I swear he is always on point.

"Hey y'all!" He yells out as he enters the house.

"Kareem, I noticed 2 cars sitting outside in the cul-de-sac. Were they there when you pulled up?"

"Yep, and they gone be there until I lay my hands on De'Angelo ass. I'm guessing that combo at the wedding wasn't enough. He must think it's ok to call and talk reckless to you. I guarantee that muthafucka gone learn this time. So, until I cancel his subscription to you, the cars will be on standby to keep y'all safe in the event that I can't always get here. I gotta go back to work, and I don't get off til 3AM. I may be back out here, but it all depends on the progress at the job. But, I may just go home and go to sleep."

I ask, "Did you take care of that situation with Mya?"

"You called it out. She couldn't keep her lie straight. I still gotta get the rest of my stuff from over there. But, yeah she put that shit together and she had the nerve to bitch and fuss when I didn't come that night. So, yeah, you were right."

He leaned in to kiss me on my forehead. I swear he is the most sensitive thug you'll ever wanna meet.

"One more question before you go, does the name Horisha ring a bell?"

"Yep, did she call you today?"

"Yeah, and she called on line 4. That's what piqued my interest because only a few people know to call on line 4. Who is she? Why is she calling me?"

"Did you talk to her?"

"No, because I wasn't sure who she was. So, I had Ronnie take a message."

"She's safe. Call her."

"Well, who is she and what does she want with me?"

"She has the answers to all your questions Lil' One. Tomorrow be sure to call her back. Y'all be safe tonight. I'll call you tonight to let you know what I decide to do."

Finally, a night of relaxation with my boys. Surprisingly, there's no company over, and both of them are in their own world. But, we're all in the same room silently spending time with one another.

As I rudely interrupted the stale air, "Hey let's have a silent party?"

Ryan replied, "That'll be great, but who's going to be our DJ?"

"Um, excuse me, we can DJ our own music. We all have headphones, we all have iPhones. Therefore, we can play whatever upbeat music we want. We can dance, release some stress, and rock out for 3- 5 minutes before we go to bed."

"If you insist, then I guess I'll kick it with the OG for the one time. Dino, go grab our headphones, so we can beat our OG in this dance party."

Excitedly, Dino ran to grab the headphones and came back. We were able to connect our devices to the headphones and the three of us had a silent party in the living room. I'm unsure of what they listened to. By the way they were dancing, Dino had to be playing either Michael Jackson, Justin Bieber, or Usher. Now Ryan, that's a different story, he amazes me with his choice of music. He could've been anywhere in the Temptation era all the way to the new group Bottum up. With Toolii being his latest hip hop inspiration, then I'll have to go with Bottum up. As for me, I'm a ballroom kinda girl, so my favorite ballroom song is Lucy Pearl's "Dance Tonight". I know this is exactly what I needed, fun times with my boys, and creating memories while we can. With quarantine life, it's been crazy. But now, I can just let my hair down and be mommy. As the music played, we looked at each other, pointed, laughed and partied as if no one else cared.

Chapter 6

The Office

I know last night was exactly what I needed, fun with the boys, a good night's rest, and a packed schedule for today. First, I'll go throw something together for breakfast, pick out my clothes, shower, and head to the office. I swear, I'm going to get my own real estate company and be able to work from home; if I feel like it or do it however I see fit. This being someone else's top realtor is not cutting it for me anymore. But, it pays the bills so until I put all my ducks in a row to be able to do this on my own, I'm going to take my ass to work for these other people.

Just finished breakfast, and even put some red beans in the crock pot for later. Damn, it's amazing what a good night's rest will do to you. Today, I think I'll just be super casual. A jogging suit will do today. Now of course, I can't wear tennis shoes, but heels make anything look good. I'll wear my Louis Vuitton heels I just got, courtesy of Lance Whitaker. Shit, shower, and shave, then I'm out the door.

Either the water pressure in the shower was different today, or I was extremely horny. The way the water was hitting my nipples gave me a feeling I hadn't felt before. So naturally, I turned the shower head to the massage cycle and let it stimulate my clitoris region. Whether you are single or not, I don't care what anyone has to say, but being able to have a shower head with multiple settings is a must have. The way the water pressure came out of the shower head and the circular motion I used to rub my love below was just right. The temperature of the water was perfect. My hand to clit pressure ratio was on point. Before I knew it, I was standing there having a single session with myself in the shower.

Talk about a perfect way to start the day. I swear I can please myself better than anyone else, but having someone else do it is always more delightful. As I was enjoying myself, I found myself fantasizing about a session I had a few years back. We fucked in the shower. We had anal sex. I know it wasn't the best for him, but he did it because that's what I like. Nevertheless, as I'm thinking about that, I started to finger my wet pussy and enjoy all the stimulation I was getting in the shower. Playing with my pussy, thinking about him fucking me in my ass, all while in the water gave me an orgasm out of this world. I even had the nerve to call his name. I hope my ancestors don't send his ass my way, because I really was not trying to manifest anything. I just got caught up in the moment. But the way my ancestors are set up, he'll be showing up real soon.

Stepping out the shower and to see my own wet, sexy body turned me on again. I don't know if it's just me or am I looking good? The melanin is popping, the vitamin D got me sun kissed and glowing. Damn Isis, let's go take a few nude pics, send them to Kareem, and let's see what type of reaction you get.

Leaving the house, I'm headed to the office, but first I need to stop and get gas. I swear I hate going to the gas station. Nevertheless, this car isn't going to make it unless I make this small detour. Enjoying the fresh morning sunshine, and the breeze, I couldn't help but to start bobbin' my head back and forth to the radio. When you look good, and feel good, good music just does something to you. I truly think I was a trap queen in my former life.

Pulling up to the gas station, I couldn't help but to notice someone that looks like little Miss Kupenda. As I get closer to the pump, I see that it is her. I wonder what slick shit she may try to pull. I know she knows who I am, shit, the nail salon, the wedding, the Louis Vuitton store, the bar, and not to mention Ronnie. Besides, Avery bought that condominium building that she was living in and ultimately put her ratchet ass out, so now, where is she living? Maybe she won't say anything to me, she already knows my clap back game is strong.

Entering the gas station, I hear her goofy ass laugh while she's on the phone, and by the time she looks up and notices it's me, all she could say was, "Bitch, let me call you back."

"Well, hello Kupenda!"

"Isis, look before you start getting all bourgeois and shit, just know I'm not trying to start no trouble, but you should know that I think that was some fucked up shit you did at my auntie wedding. Yeah, I know all about you and De'Angelo but to do that bullshit at the wedding was just classless and egregious."

Before she could finish, I politely interrupted her. The universe must have had me in mind when they set this up, I've been waiting to pay her back for all the mess that she's done to me. Hell, I had to get rid of my damn blouse from the wine stain. I couldn't get out from her bumping my chair and making me spill it on me. Nevertheless, here's my opportunity.

"Egregious, now that's a big word for someone who sleeps with other peoples' husbands. Isn't that the pot calling the kettle black? Listen little Miss Kupenda, first and foremost, I am grown as hell and the actions I display are truly that of a grown ass woman. Unlike yourself, frolicking around with other people's husbands, how about you come down to the real estate office, fill out an application with one of the realtors, so you can work under them, save some money, get your credit up to par, and buy your own shit. It's about owning stuff and having things in your own name, so when the wife of the man your fucking finds out about you, purchases the building you live in and puts your ass out, you won't be at the gas station this early in the morning with a bonnet, a tank top, pajama pants, Ugg slides, and no lashes. Come on, baby girl, take a few lessons from me. Get your head in the game, don't be the game. The game always gets played. Be the player. The game is called Chess, not Checkers."

I stopped engaging with her and told the attendant I needed to fill up number 9, threw him a blueberry, turned around, tapped her on her shoulder, winked, told her to get it together, and I walked away.

I truly know this is not the last of her, and I'll know how much I've affected her once I get to the office and hear it from Ronnie. Meanwhile, let me pump this gas, go get my change, so I can get to work. This little dog head ass bitch got me fucked up. I'm having a good morning, and I'm going to continue it. But I must call Avery and give her this tea. Pulling up to the office, I call Avery, but she doesn't answer. No need to leave a message, she'll see a missed call and call me back.

Entering the office, Ronnie hands me a cup of hot rose & chamomile tea.

"Good morning, Boss Lady, I see you're looking fantastic, and smelling delightful. What's gotten into you today? Have you had a bowl of un-peed in cheerios?"

We laugh and begin to go over the events for the day.

"Here are your messages for this morning. I've been here since 9 and Horisha has called again. Have you checked who she is and what she wants?"

"No, I haven't, but I did ask Kareem. He said she'll have all the answers to the questions I have. Ronnie, I'll call her after lunch. I'm still trying to figure out what it is she wants with me. Kareem said she's safe. So, yeah, I honestly don't know, so she's going to have to wait until after lunch."

Sitting at my desk seriously pondering whether or not to call this woman back, Kareem told me she's safe, and I trust him wholeheartedly, but what does she want with me?

I sit back and think about all the things I need to do today, it was at that moment that I heard a bunch of commotion coming from the hallway.

"Ronnie, is everything all right out there?"

"Boss Lady, come get this nigga off me!"

I quickly start to run into the office and see what the commotion is all about. Then I hear something crash up against the door of my office.. Upon opening the door, I couldn't help but to see Ronnie in the corner between the file cabinet and the window struggling to breath because he's being choked by De'Angelo. Having to react quickly, I hit his ass so hard in his neck that it temporarily caused him to loosen his hold of Ronnie and stumble to the floor.

As Ronnie struggles to regain his breath, I go over to the phone and quickly call security to let them know there's been a disturbance in my office. Meanwhile, I check on Ronnie. Once I realize that Ronnie's doing fine, I focus my attention on this coward-ass bastard that had the nerve to come to my office and try to mess with my assistant.

Angrily, I ask, "What in the fuck are you doing in my office? Better question, how the fuck did you make it past security? Didn't you endure enough embarrassment this weekend? Why are you even bothering us? Oh I know, you can't get yo' dick sucked by little boys no more. You ain't getting no pussy at home, or is it the fact that you aint realized that fat meat is greasy. You really think I'm fucking playing with you? De'Angelo, you know damn well I ain't the one to be played with. You know shit is about to get thick for yo' ass when Kareem finds out what type of stunt you just pulled."

Attempting to get his bearings he manages to mumble the words, "Fuck you, Bitch. All that tough talking you doing ain't phasing me. You know how I gets down."

Walking over to the file cabinet, I opened the third drawer and pulled out my Smith and Wesson .40 caliber handgun. I cocked it and pointed it at his head.

I politely said, "I told you that you had one more time to call me a bitch..."

Before I could finish my sentence, security came into the office just in time for me to act as if I was in total danger.

Screaming, "Get him out of here! This man is insane. I want him arrested for assault. Get him out of here now."

Once the security officers apprehended him and took him away, I had to make sure that Ronnie was alright before I made a decision to close shop or carry on with the day.

I know Ronnie is a tough cookie, but this incident hit too close to home. I actually saw Ronnie in a very vulnerable state and he was inconsolable. I just told him to go to the restroom. I wanted him to try to gather himself and to take all the time he needed.

Looking at the front office, it's not a complete mess, but it's messy enough. So, let me attempt to get stuff back in order before the partners come up here and I have to lie about what just took place. I can't figure out why the hell De'Angleo would bring that shit to my office. Who am I kidding, I thought his ass would've been here the next day with his stupid ass. Anywho, he knows damn well I'm the pepper in the salt around this bitch, and anything I do that's not with the flow of the office, they're gonna wanna have my ass on a silver platter. I really gotta get my own shit, not just because of this shit, but just so I don't have all those other people in my business. Cleaning up the mess, I hear a familiar voice coming from the hallway.

"Good morning, Isis Carrington, is everything alright in here? Do I need to call the crew?"

Laughing cutely, I replied, "No. I think I've got it handled, thank you."

As I look over my shoulder, I notice Lance Whitaker is standing in my office, if things couldn't get any more bizarre.

"Well, what do I owe the pleasure of this visit? Buying anymore condos? We both laughed.

He simply replied, "No, I'm not buying any more condos, I was actually in the area and I wanted to stop by to just say, 'thank you'"

"I'm not following."

"Thank you for not telling Avery about the bullshit I was on with the condos and the check/ You know all my tomfooleries."

Laughing out loud, "I appreciate your thank you, I guess. But, I'm wondering how many people use the word, *tomfooleries*. You are so extra, Mr. Whitaker. But, for real, I am developing a friendship with Avery and I wouldn't want to hurt her. But, just so you know, she's on yo' ass, so whatever you are doing, or aren't doing, you need to clean that shit up and do it expeditiously. She's on to you. I can't and won't violate our friendship code, but I will say this, don't fuck around and lose your diamond chasing rhinestones."

"You're right, Isis, and I'm going to be a better husband to Avery and an even better dad to Aniya. Sometimes my shenanigans gets the best of me and these ladies be throwing themselves at me and oftentimes I get caught slipping, you don't got to say it, I'm a mess."

"Aht, Aht, Aht, don't you say shit else. I don't wanna be in the middle of the shit between you and Avery because I'll be forced to tell her what I know."

Still laughing, I told him that he has a wonderful family and he needs to protect them at all cost.

Then, I questioned him.

Now seriously, "Why are you in my office? Let me guess, you talked to Kupenda this morning and she told you I saw her at the gas station?"

"I did speak with her, but she didn't tell me she saw you at all."

"Hmmm, now that's weird. She never mentioned me?"

I'm thinking maybe my smart-ass clap back gave her something to think about.

"Well then spill it. Again, why are you in my office?"

"Listen, Isis, I fucked up big time this time, and I'm trying to straighten it out before Avery finds out. But, I'm running out of time and I don't know what to do."

"Aww shit, Lance, I don't want to be in the middle of any of this shit. I got enough shit on my plate to deal with, and do you see my office? I gotta handle my own scandal before I even attempt to try to help somebody else sort out theirs. So, please if you don't mind, don't say another word, I really don't wanna be involved. Now, if you'll excuse me, I need to finish cleaning this mess up and go check on Ronnie. You can see yourself out."

Before I could push past him to go check on Ronnie, he yells out, "I been fucking the neighbor's nanny."

I was in total disgust, as I slammed down the stuff I was picking up off the floor.

"Shit, Lance, didn't I just tell you I didn't want to know. Now you know that places me in a fucked-up situation with Avery. Besides, why are you telling me? What the fuck do I got to do with you fucking the neighbor's nanny? Shit, nigga, you just keep downgrading. You fucking with the 'help'!"

As I angrily push past him I tell him again, "Let yourself out."

"Isis, wait, you have to hear me out, it's deeper than you know. That's why I'm here. I need to talk to someone, so I can hear another person's perspective."

"As much as I don't want to hear this shit, I'm giving you 10 minutes, and whatever you don't get out in those 10 minutes, oh fucking well. Go have a seat in my office. I'm going to check on Ronnie, I'll be right back."

Exiting my office, I'm literally blown away. I can't believe what just happened in a matter of 20 minutes. De'Angelo got past security and jumped on Ronnie with attempts to get to me. Lance shows up confessing his thottish ways, as if Avery doesn't know, and to top it off, he confides in me, putting me in a fucked up situation because I'm friends with Avery. Now wait a minute, if I play my cards right, then this new real estate office might be well within my reach. But wait, this nigga ain't the man behind the money. Shit! I gotta figure out which route to take because all this information that just fell in my lap is truly confirmation.

Snapping out of my mental rewind, I bump into Ronnie.

"Baby, are you alright? Do you need anything? I'm so sorry. He's being dealt with by security and I'm sure the police will want statements to see if we want to press charges."

It's clear that he's still shaken up and with him being so yellow, you can see the red marks around his neck, his poor eyes are red and swollen from crying. He just looks so distraught.

"Boss Lady, can I go home?"

"You don't think you're staying in my office today to keep reliving this incident. Yes, please go home. But, first can you go to urgent care, have them examine you, and take photos. This way when we do decide to press charges, we'll have that part already handled."

With a shaky voice he replied, "Yes".

"Don't worry about the mess. I'll handle that just go and I'll call and check on you later."

Heading back to the office, I detoured to the head realtor's office to see what he knows, if anything.

"Good morning, Mr. Donahue, let me explain what just happened upstairs."

Before I could spill the beans on myself, he had already been tipped off by security.

"No need to explain. I saw the security footage. I already have the movers ready at the end of the day to pack up your stuff and..."

"Wait, pack up my stuff? I'm being fired?"

"If you let me finish, I'm moving you out of that office to another suite. I can't risk Ronnie being assaulted again. Honestly, no one needs to come to their place of work and see the place their assault took place. So when you leave today, don't have any worries. We'll have you moved and set up in a new suite for work in the morning."

With tears in my eyes, "Thank you, I don't know what to say. I really appreciate you for looking out for Ronnie like this. Your thoughtfulness means so much. I'm sure he'll be happy when he finds out about the new location. Thank you so much."

As I'm leaving his office, headed back to mine, I can't help but to feel a bit of relief about the situation. Now, let me get my head on straight to be able to tackle this bullshit that Lance is getting ready to lay on me. Hopefully, he's left my office, but hell knowing him, he's still sitting his ass in there.

I was right. He's still sitting in my office.

"Ok, the clock starts now. You have 10 minutes to get everything you need to tell me off your chest, and you better have a damn good reason why I shouldn't share this tea with Avery."

"Listen, her name is NuNuu. I saw her while I was out with Kupenda one night. Kupenda starts telling me who she is and how the two of them don't like each other. Apparently, the two of them at some point dated the same guy, and you know how that goes."

Trying not to give a fuck, I blurted out, "Ok, so how did you end up fucking the NuNuu chick?"

"Well, I saw her at the store a few times, and every time I saw her, I couldn't get her out of my head. Then, I found out that she is the neighbor's nanny in the backyard. A few times we ended up chatting at the fence, then she gave me her number and the rest is history."

"So, you just go around fucking the help. I can't deal with you today, Listen, either you gone tell Avery what's good, or you gone cut this NuNuu chic off. Those are the only two choices you have, unless there's something you are not telling me. Honestly, you didn't need my perspective on this. I truly think you are still hiding some shit but that is not my concern; I've literally had enough for one day.

As he stands up to leave, he says "You're right. There's more. But, I don't want to overwhelm you anymore than you already are."

"You are already spilling beans, go ahead, and get to talking. This day can't possibly get any crazier."

"Before I met Avery, I dealt with this one woman. We used to do dirt together, and she was a good girl. I was the street nigga. I got into some trouble and she took the bid for me. It's been almost 20 years. She was just released from prison, and she is looking for the money that I was supposed to save for her for taking the bid."

"Just asking, but how much money is she supposed to have waiting for her when she gets home?"

"Shit, about 50 grand."

"Damn, Lance, you got some shit stirring. When is she looking to collect her bread?"

"ASAP, but in order for me to get this money without Avery finding out I need you to help me find a property for the low. I want you to help me flip it real quick, so I can get the money without Avery knowing. Then, I can get this woman off my back."

"And that's the bombshell I was looking for. I knew it was something you needed me for because your ass just don't show up needing a fucking perspective. Who is this little prison bird you getting ready to pay off? I need to know all the details, so I can sleep on this before I can give you an answer on whether I want to be involved in your fuckery."

KeanaMonique

"Her name is Horisha McFadden. She is 39. She went to prison at 19. She was a first-time offender, but they made an example out of her. They gave her the max for what we did. She was released about a week ago from Aldridge State Penitentiary for Women."

Chapter 7

The Office

Talk about flabbergasted, I'm completely blown away. I gotta get Kareem on the phone when to share this mess I, lightweight, straightened out. Now, this is unbelievable. The dots have somewhat been connected, but yet I'm still wondering what she wants with me? I don't think Kareem knows of Lance or the connection, so I gotta tread lightly when I talk to him just to see what he knows.

Let me just call her back first. As the phone is ringing, I'm sitting here in total disbelief about what I just found out. I swear the universe just drops stuff in my lap like nobody's business.

"Hello"

"Hi, this is Isis Carrington. I'm returning a call to Horisha."

"Well, hi there, Ms. Carrington. Is it ok if I call you that?"

"Isis will do fine, thank you, how may I help you?"

"I am childhood friends with Kareem. He gave me your number to see if you could possibly assist me in gaining employment."

“Well first off, I’m a realtor, and I’m unsure what I can help you with. Are you a real estate agent? Do you type and need an assistant type of job?”

“Oh no, I’m sorry. I passed the licensing exam before I got out of prison.”

“I’m sorry. Did you say prison? If I may ask, how long were you locked up?”

As she further explains, “I did close to 20 years. I went away when I was 19 years old and spent the first half of my life locked up for something I didn’t do. But, since the other party involved refused to take accountability for their actions, I did all the time. But, that’s a story for another day.”

“Yes, I’m sorry. I didn't mean to pry. Well since you’ve passed the exam, you're one step closer to obtaining employment. I just have a few questions. Are you looking to work right now? Are you in a position to wait? I’m only asking because I’m just a partner here at this real estate office, but I’m looking to get my own firm within the next few months. I need to know which way to direct you.”

“I would like to start working now, and maybe I can shadow you. This way when you get your own office, I can work at your place of business.”

"Well, go to keysrealestate.com and upload your resume under careers and put my name in the subject section, so I can get it and direct it to Mr. Donahue. We can get you scheduled for an interview, but with COVID-19 he may or may not have to hold the interview via Zoom. Will that be okay for you?"

"Yes, that'll work just fine. I'm about to do it right now. Thank you for this helpful information."

"No problem. If you need anything just let me know, you have my number, and I'm always a call away. Have a great day."

"Thank you! You also."

Now, I bet you $1.00 to a bucket of shit, Kareem is going to tell me that he knew all of this information, but since it wasn't his information to pass, then he couldn't say anything. The phone hadn't even made a complete cycle in ring tones before he picked it up.

"What's up, lil momma? Have you talked to Horisha?"

"We actually just got off the phone. She is looking for a job in the real estate business, and wanted to know if I could help her out. But, you know this ain't my shit, so I told her to apply online, submit her resume, and we'll go from there. So now that she's told me the reason for her call, tell me what she did to go to prison."

With a deep exhale, Kareem starts to explain, "Ma, she went on some bullshit, this lame ass nigga had her moving weight and she didn't know. She was in transit and got pulled over. The nigga told her to go switch vehicles with somebody and come right back. Well, apparently somebody tipped off the 'dem boys. They pulled her over and asked if they could search the car. Shit, she didn't know what was going on so she said, 'yeah'. They found 6 kilos in the trunk around the spare tire, and a few more in the dashboard. It was about 9 in total, I think. So, they gave her 2 years per kilo."

"Well damn, who is this lame ass nigga that set her up?"

"Some lame, she wouldn't give me his name. After all these years, she's still protecting him. So, I don't know too much about him just yet."

"Why did she say something about him?"

"Nope. I didn't ask. I didn't think it was my business. I'll pry more when she has her interview."

"How do you know she gone be called for an interview?"

"Because, I'm Isis Muthafuckin' Carrington, and I said what I said."

We started laughing and just before we ended our conversation, I had to drop the bomb on him.

"DeAngelo came up here today, got past security, and jumped on Ronnie, I hit him in the neck, pulled out my piece, and held him until security got here. My office will be transferred in the morning, and Ronnie is at urgent care getting looked at before this goes to the police."

"This nigga done got too damn close, I'm on his head. I tried to warn that nigga, but he fucking with the wrong one. Are you okay?"

"Yeah, I'm good. I was more concerned with Ronnie and I sent him home right after the incident. I still have yet to go check on him."

"I'm telling you now, you not gone like what I do next. So gone head and cuss me out, roll yo' neck and do whatever it is you do with your hands, 'cause I'm not stopping until I'm satisfied."

Laughing, I replied, "That sounds like sex."

"Get off my phone. I'll get up with you later."

Damn, I love him. He gets on my nerves, but he always comes through for me, no matter what it is.

He is truly my best friend. I can't help but wonder what his version of satisfaction looks like?

After the events of today, I really just want to go home, but I know I can't. I need to see what all Ronnie had on his to do list. At least, I can get started and keep these balls rolling. Shuffling through the mess on Ronnie's desk, the phone rings.

"Isis speaking, how can I help you?"

"Oh, damn, I wasn't expecting you to answer the phone. Where's Ronnie?"

"I'm sorry to disappoint you, but who's speaking?"

"This is Kupenda."

"Kupenda, Ronnie is gone for the day. You may be able to catch him on his cell phone. Is there anything else I can help you with?"

"Naw, I'll try his phone."

"Kupenda, did you have an opportunity to drop off your resume here at the office?"

I was giggling so hard on the inside, but I had to keep my composure.

"Hell naw, but since you asking like you care, I just might."

"Aht aht aht, don't think that. I just know you have to be gainfully employed before you secure housing."

In typical Kupenda fashion, she hung up. I needed that. Shit, my cheerios already peed in for the day, so why not pee in someone else's. Fuck her.

Chapter 8

The Office

I wonder why I haven't heard from Avery. She's really good at calling me back. I hope nothing happened to her, or maybe she found out all about Lance's bullshit and she knows I know. Is that why she hasn't called me back yet? It could be I'm just thinking too hard. It is what I do, but hey maybe she is just busy. I just know I can't be obsessing about why Avery hasn't called me back. I have too much on my plate, but she and I are honing in on a friendship. I need to just give her a fair shot, and actually be open to friendship.

While waiting for a few things to happen, I need to finish getting stuff together and get set up for the movers. So, I can be transferred. Mr. Donahue is the best. I really appreciate him for moving my office, so that Ronnie is safe and feels safe. I wonder what he'll do when he gets the news that I'm leaving. I'm giving myself about 8 months, then I'm out of here.

Dancing in the office to songs in my mind, I get distracted by the movers knocking at the door.

"Hi, we're here to transfer you from this floor to the top floor penthouse office."

"Wait, you mean to tell me Mr. Donahue is giving me the penthouse suite for my office? You know that's the one that overlooks the city right?"

"You are Isis Carrington, right?"

"The one and only, why do you ask?"

"The moving requisition states that Isis Carrington is to be moved from her current location to the penthouse office at the top floor."

"Stop playing with my emotions, let me see that form."

I'll be damned. Sure as shit, it says transfer to the penthouse office suite. Now why is Mr. Donahue being this generous to Ronnie and I? I swear he knows I'm about to leave him, and he's doing the most so that I'll stick around. Shake it off girl, there you go always thinking the worst.

"Ma'am, if you'll excuse us, we need to get you moved."

"Pardon me, I'm sorry. Do I need to pack any of this stuff up?"

"No, actually you can leave it all right where it's at and we'll take care of the rest."

"In that case, I'm leaving for the day. But wait, where are the keys to my new office?"

"I'm sorry, Ms. Carrington, there are no keys to the office. It's a keyless entry. You can either set up your fingerprint, or use a pin number. But, there are no keys."

"Oh, well I'll set a pin number. Where's the information on how to do it?"

He passed me a sheet of paper with the prompts on how to do it and I proceeded to leave the office.

I wonder what's behind all this extra niceness. I know it, damn sure, ain't Ronnie's safety, especially the top office. All this time, I've only heard of what the office looks like, now it's getting ready to be mine. This is unreal. Something's strange, and if I know anything, I know the universe will show and prove.

"Pick up the phone Ronnie."

Voicemail? Well damn, he better be at the urgent care 'cause he doesn't ever not answer my phone call.

Headed to my car, my phone rings. In my hurry to check on Ronnie, I just answered it.

"Ronnie, are you okay? Where are you?"

"I'm certainly not Ronnie, and I'm driving home, after a long day. What's going on with you?"

"Avery, girl this day has been so upside down. It's pathetic. I won't even begin to tell you what happened today."

She let out the most sinister laugh I had ever heard before.

Then she says, "Well you do know what today is right?"

"Um Thursday, is that supposed to mean anything?"

"Not only is it Thursday, but it's a new moon, and not only is it new, but it's gonna be full. So, the energies of people are running rampant and it's the end of the Mercury retrograde."

As I let out a sigh of relief, she replied, "Well, I'll be damned. All that happened today, and it's still daylight outside. I can only imagine what will happen tonight. What's going on with you?"

"Shit, girl, I think we've narrowed down all of Niya's prom / graduation stuff. Be thankful you have boys because all this unnecessary shit is for the birds."

We both laughed and then, she said, "Any leads on the situation?"

And since she brought it up, I couldn't lie, but I'll only tell her what Ronnie told me. I'll leave Lance's bullshit for later.

"Well since you asked before I could tell you, check this out, the little trollop as you so affectionately called her, does in fact have some dealings with Lance, what those dealings are as of right now, I'm not sure. But, I know this to be true because my assistant, Ronnie, told me that NuNuu and Kupenda do not get along and to make a long story even shorter, Kupenda started messing with NuNuu's baby daddy. So once NuNuu found out, she sought out revenge on her baby daddy as well as Kupenda. So, where Lance fits into all of this is still unknown and I'm working on it, but I'm going to need a few more days. Sorry to be the bearer of bad news."

She lets out that laugh again, "Girl ain't that some shit, but the bitch in the backyard tho. I mean damn he is playing too close to home. I appreciate the information, and don't worry about the rest. That's confirmation enough."

"Ok, now wait, we're not too sure that he's dealing with the trollop just yet, so we still need to confirm that."

Avery explains, “My gut tells me he is, so I’m going to take that as enough confirmation. Let the chips fall where they may.

One thing for sure, two things for certain:

1. He always does something stupid that shows his hand

and exposes his fuckery.

2. So now, all I have to do is wait. I’m going to have fun doing it.”

“I’m really scared to ask what that means, but what the hell? What does that mean?”

“No, it’s not that bad. It only means that I’m gonna keep him on pins and needles until the opportunity comes up and he shows his hand.”

“I mean, can you be that patient and wait it out?” “Again, one thing about my husband is it won’t take long at all. Trust me.”

I laugh. “Well in that case, let the fun begin.”

“Now, tell me about your crazy day.”

“For starters, De’Angelo got past security and put his hands on Ronnie. Ronnie got sent home for the day with strict instructions to go to the urgent care and then to the police station. That's why when you called, I called you Ronnie because I had just tried to call him and he didn't answer. Then, the owner of the firm got wind of the mess and out of the goodness of his heart, he transferred my office to the penthouse suite on the top floor, and then, I had an unexpected past client drop by looking to flip some real estate. In a nutshell, that's how my day went. I'm still trying to figure out when I'm going to put the ball in motion to start to find my own space. I really want my own firm. I feel like if I don't move on this process quickly, then I may just be working here forever."

"Ok, now did you say you want to find your own space?," Avery asks.

"Yeah, I did say that, but I have to strategically plan for that big financial move. Now is not the best time with Ryan being a senior and all."

Avery pauses and then says, "Let's make a deal, since you are the real estate agent. You find an area that you think your office would thrive in. Show it to me. I'll put a bid in on it, buy it, and lease it to you for 6 months. Then, I'll just deed it over to you."

"Whoa! I can't let you do that. That's a big financial step you're taking with this. Shouldn't you talk to your husband first?"

"Girl, you don't listen to shit I say to you. I make the world go round over here in my neighborhood. Besides, I need to invest in more property, so I can make a smooth transition. Don't ask me anything else until I see you in person. Actually, right now I've got another call coming in. I'll call you back."

The call was terminated.

She sure does have a weird way of ending calls. No talk to you later, girl bye, no nothing. She just hangs up. I'm gonna have to tell her that is rude. But, hell, knowing her, she'll probably tell me to get over it and keep it moving. Laughing to myself, the cell phone starts to ring.

"Hello, this is Isis speaking."

"Boss lady, it's me. I'm leaving urgent care, and heading to the police station."

At that moment, I was able to breathe a sigh of relief,

"Oh my goodness, Ronnie, I'm so sorry this happened to you. Just know that Mr. Donahue got wind of it and he moved our office to the penthouse suite. So, you'll be safe and won't be uncomfortable while you work."

"Well alright then, Tristan Donahue, look at you doing big things. Wait a minute, why is he moving us to the penthouse, Boss Lady you haven't told him you're not gonna be there too much longer have you?"

In a disappointed voice I replied, "No, Ronnie I couldn't bring myself to say those words without having a solid back up plan in motion, and speaking of motion, I'll have more information about that real soon. So, don't worry about that. What did they say at urgent care?"

"They x-rayed my face, neck and back. It looks negative, but until the radiologist reads them, they can't be sure. Now, I'm headed to the police station to file a complaint," Ronnie explains.

"Oh ok, that's good to hear, and just to let you know Kupenda called the office looking for you. She said she'd call your cell phone. Just giving you the heads up."

"Yeah, she sent me a text."

"Boss Lady, must you constantly pick on her?"

Sarcastically speaking, I say, "This is for what she had been doing to me every time she saw me, she had it coming. But, I'll lay off her for a while. Well, at least until the opportunity presents itself again."

“Now you know the former first lady said, “When they go low, we go high”. So for real, you know you got her beat. Can you just let her slide? For me, please?”

“Alright, alright, only for you. But, the guilt trip you are trying to lay on me, lay it on her as well. I don’t wanna be the only one being disciplined here.”

We both let out a laugh. He continued to tell me about how he felt about today’s events.

“Listen Ronnie, I know you are having a hard time digesting the past couple of hours, and it won’t just be a get over it type of situation. So, if you need to take a few days and regroup, then I’ll completely understand.”

He burst out in laughter.

“Look B, I’m a tough cookie and if you think what DeAngelo did is gone have me losing my money, then you got another thing coming. Besides if you even think twice that I’m gone let you run the front office, then, yeah you might need to have that head of yours examined.”

“Excuse me, I'm still your boss. I was just concerned, and just for the record, I can run my own office.”

"You know I meant no real harm by that, but I truly know you can do it alone. Honestly, I'm good. Anywho, I hate to cut the conversation short, but I'm pulling up at the police station. I'll keep you posted."

"Ok, bye."

Chapter 9

Isis & Avery

I need a drink. Ronnie is hurt. DeAngelo has lost his fucking mind. Lance is tripping and Avery's calmness is making me nervous. I just want to get away, crawl under somebody's rock, and take a few days to myself. I need my children, but hell, my house just might be full of other people's children. Let's just hope today ain't one of those days.

Driving home, I decided to stop at The Blue Room. I need something good to eat and a nice drink. The Blue Room is a small intimate restaurant with the bomb food. I really just want some cajun fries and a hurricane. My mind is going ape shit. The circumstances of today's events are mind boggling. I really can't make this shit up. But the weird part about everything is, I'm still winning. I couldn't do anything but laugh to myself, I'm winning. Out of all the shenanigans of today, Isis Carrington still came out on top. How? Might you ask, because I ended up with the penthouse office suite at my job.

Walking into The Blue Room, the clouds looked unusually blue. Now of course, it's odd to have blue clouds over The Blue Room, but it's a different kind of vibe here. I wouldn't expect anything less than unusual. As I entered, my phone started ringing and you could hear a crowd of people using all types of vulgarities. Now, it is not strange that you hear people cursing, but wait a moment, it's too much going on.

Making my way to be seated, I happened to gaze over at the big screen television and who do I see, Lance Whitaker. It appears to be an old photo of Lance, but still it is in fact, Lance. Now why in the hell is his face plastered all over the news.

"Excuse me, what's on the TV?"

The hostess responded, "Girl, I don't know, some man from around here had some chick take a bid for him on some big dope case almost 20 years ago. The news found her and tried to interview her, but she's not answering any questions. Girl, I was barely listening."

She just gave the damn rundown for someone not to have been paying attention. As I make my way to my seat, I get my phone out and see a missed call from Avery. Now, I'm really scared because if this just hit the news, Avery just called me, then it's a clear indication that she knows about Horisha and Lance.

The hostess lady extended her hand and said, "Follow me this way to your seat."

"If I may, can I be seated in a booth please?"

"Sure, right this way," the hostess responds with a smile.

I return Avery's call while I am being seated in the booth.

"Hey girl I missed your call, what's going on?"

"Hey, yeah, where are you?" Avery asked as if she's in a rush. "I need to pull up real fast."

"I actually just got to The Blue Room to have a drink."

"Are you alone?"

"Yep. Pull up. I'm in a booth. Just tell the hostess you're here to see me."

Now, I gotta make this quick. As I'm seated in my booth, being low key, I honestly don't know how much time I have until Avery gets here. I really hadn't planned on being with anyone at this moment. I don't get to do this in public too often, but now I gotta rush and get it done.

The waitress interrupts my thoughts by saying, "Ma'am, can I get you anything to drink while you look over your menu?"

"I'll take a top shelf hurricane with cherries and pineapples."

The minute she walked away, I went straight for my purse and grabbed my lipstick vibrator. I untied my jogging pants, slid my panties to the side, turned it on, and placed it right on top of my clitoris. I just sat there and let it do its thing.

As I laid my head back and took a moment to enjoy this public masturbation session, everything else seemed non-essential. The quietness of the vibrator is amazing. Now, if I can only lift my head up to make it seem as if I'm paying attention I don't need this to be too obvious. This moment is so satisfying and I know the orgasm will be amazing. I just have to find something to fixate my focus on, so my memory can take me to a place of pure enjoyment.

The attention this toy is giving my clitoris is amazing. The fact that it's not moving and I can have both my hands free, so I can appear normal is heightening my experience. Staring off into space, I begin thinking about the time Kareem popped up on me in the restaurant while I was with Jaylen. This is the scene playing in my mind. I really need him to eat this pussy like he did back then. As I am thinking about releasing my juice all over his beard is the exact moment I released all my juice on me.

I can't shake off this feeling. I just have to sit here and let it pass. For whatever reason, I came pretty quickly. Is it because I'm stressed? Is it because I'm in the restaurant trying to have a private moment in a public place? Was it the pressure to finish before the waitress or Avery gets here? Just as I'm over the orgasm, I remove the toy from my gateway. Here comes the waitress with my drink. Talk about perfect timing. As soon as Avery arrives, I can go wash my hands and clean myself up. Thank goodness, I keep wet wipes in my purse.

The waitress asks, "Are you ready to order?"

"No, not right now. I'm waiting for my guest to get here. But, you can sit my drink right here, thank you."

"No problem. I'll check on you in a few moments when your guest arrives."

"You know what? Bring me another top shelf hurricane and with this one add a shot on the side. I think she has some stuff she needs to talk about."

We both laughed and she walked away.

As I'm figuring out how to adjust my panties, Avery walks in.

"Girl, I'm so glad. I was literally around the corner. I was about to blow a gasket. Have you heard the latest news on my trifling-ass husband? This nigga is making me look bad."

"Um, have a seat please. It looks like you are chastising me."

We both laughed.

That was the least I could do to soften the situation because she looks pissed off. Now, I just gotta act surprised at the information she is about to give me. If I know her like I think I do, then nothing gets past her. She already knows the ins and outs of what he doesn't think she knows.

"Girl, I'm tripping. Where's our waitress? I need a drink like ASAP."

Before she could finish her sentence, here comes our waitress with her drink.

"Alright now, ladies, just let me know when you're ready to order. I'll be right over there. Take your time. There is no need to rush."

"How did you know I was going to need one of these?"

"The urgency in your voice said you needed something to take the edge off. Now. what's wrong?"

"Ok. Let me try to make a long story short," Avery starts.

"Ok. before you start, let me go to the ladies room." I politely excuse myself.

I was getting ready to lose my mind. I needed to wipe my lady parts. I'm glad she can sit there and sip her drink while I take care of this mess. Hopefully, it ain't as bad as it is when I'm with someone. I couldn't help but giggle to myself. I can't believe I just masturbated in a public restaurant. The good thing is no one even noticed. Entering the restroom, I go ahead and break out the cleansing cloths. Now, I can clean myself up for now, at least, until I get home. As I'm in the restroom, I hear another lady on the phone and from her conversation it appears that she's crying. Trying not to listen, we both come out of the stalls, and I wash my hands. She's wiping her face.

I look over and tell her, "Whatever it is, you're strong enough to handle it."

I dried my hands and left.

As I make it back to the table, I see Avery tapping her fingers on the table.

"Ok, let me guess, I took too long."

"Girl naw, this is starting to burn a hole in my chest. Ok. Now let me tell you what the hell just happened. Now like I said, I need to make a long story short. Before I met Lance, wasn't no real woman checking for him. He was only moving a little weight here and there. Then, I had the daddy-daughter talk and well I'll say the rest is for another story. Now, I did my research on him and knew he was dealing with some random chick named Risha, but that was just it. I couldn't find too much on her, and maybe it was because she didn't do shit. She was quiet, out of the way, and she had no real street background. He used her to move some weight. She didn't know it, got pulled over, and let the police search the car. Bottom line is, he let her take the wrap. Now, it's been 20 years and she's outta prison. She is looking for Lance to pay her for the time that was taken from her. She could've given him up, but she stood ten toes down and did her time. Rightfully so, she needs to be compensated, but where the fuck is she gone get the money from, because it sure as shit ain't coming from me."

"Whew! Well, I'll be damned. That's a lot to digest. So, does he know you know this information?"

"Girl hell naw, he thinks all the shit that happened between me and him is all his doing, I picked that nigga off some pictures my daddy showed me. My daddy told me to pick a nigga to make from the list of niggas and I picked Lance. Girl, he came with a folder with all his god-damned baggage. I know all about Lance and his shenanigans. Since my daddy was the Kingpin headed to do time, I needed to wash the money he was leaving me. Lance was the perfect person unbeknownst to him."

As I am processing Avery's story and trying to appear shocked, she continues.

"Now this old shit is all on the news because she just got released from prison. In true Lance fashion, he isn't answering his phone because he thinks I'm going to be on some bullshit, but hell, little does he know, I'm cool."

Now, I can't help but think, damn, she literally knows everything about this nigga. I'd be a damn fool to think she doesn't know that I know. But, I'm going to play it cool and let the cookie crumble. But as my granny always said, "The universe will show you what you need to see." But as soon as I came out of my trance, we're approached by the lady in the bathroom who was crying.

"I hate to bother you ma'am, but thank you for those encouraging words in the ladies' room. You're right. I will overcome this, thank you. I appreciate you. I was just in the bathroom, sharing some personal information, and I needed a word. So, thank you for speaking it into my life."

Before I could say anything in return, Avery happened to look up and said, "Hello Horisha, it's nice to finally meet you."

"Hi, I'm sorry, do we know each other?" Horisha responded.

"No, I'm afraid we don't know each other, but you know my husband, Lance Whitaker, and yes you will get past this. Have a seat. Let's discuss numbers."

Well, I'll be damned! What the fuck did the universe just drop in my lap? All this time I talked to her on the phone, I heard the story from Lance and Kareem, now Avery, hell I encouraged her in the ladies' room just being kind. Here it is. Just so happens this lady is the one and only Horisha. Can today get any more fucked up? Now, Avery wants to talk numbers. Please little girl don't sit down. The universe is showing out because sure as shit, she sat down.

Chapter 10

The Blue Room

I'm in a total state of disbelief over what just happened. Let me do a mental recap. Now, Avery knows about Lance's shenanigans with all the women. I got Horisha an interview with the company for a possible job. Horisha just came home from prison doing almost 20 years for Lance and his fuckery, and the woman in the bathroom I just happened to encourage is none other than, Horisha, herself; who happens to be sitting at the same table with Avery and myself. I swear today has been one hell of a day, and it's only half past 5.

Avery starts to speak, "First off, my name is Avery Whitaker and I'm the wife of Lance Whitaker. I know what transpired between the two of you years ago, and before you get defensive, this ain't what you think it is. However, we can do this two ways. One, we can partner up and get you this money, or two, I can be the worst bitch on the planet."

I quietly interject, "She doesn't mean that. She's really a nice person, She's just misunderstood."

Avery clarifies, "No, I'm not misunderstood. She's a bright woman. She knows what I mean. I'm saying it clear as day, and it isn't to be taken lightly or out of context."

In a mild voice, Horisha softly says, "Listen Mrs.Whitaker, I honestly don't want any parts in nothing that's going to cause me to get flagged on my parole. I have some requirements that need to be met and I'm not looking to ruffle anyone's feathers out here. I'm just trying to make sure I'm building my foundation, so I can get off these papers. Anything other than that, I'll have to respectfully decline."

Avery interrupts, "Why didn't you comment with the news when they confronted you earlier today?"

"Ma'am, I'm on parole, and I don't need any negative press. My family has been put through enough these last years about what I've done. So without me saying a word, no one can use it against me."

"Smart girl!" Avery says as she takes a sip of her drink.

I figured I better say something, so Horisha doesn't think this is a bum rush attack on her.

"So Horisha, this may be more than awkward for you, but my name is Isis Carrington. I spoke to you about the position that may be available at Keys Real Estate. Did you happen to submit the resume to the link that I gave you the other day?"

"Oh, yes, ma'am I did. I may have a Zoom or in person interview in a few days. Thank you, so much."

"Wonderful! Well, we'll just act like this event today didn't happen when you have your interview."

If looks could kill, Avery shot me a look so vicious the energy off her face burned a whole through my skin. Furthermore, the pleasantries might have been pushing Avery's buttons because she just came out of nowhere and shut it down.

"Horisha, or may I call you Risha?"

"No, you may not call me Risha. My name is Horisha, and I'd like to be addressed as such."

"Well, excuse me then, Horisha, listen, we can be very helpful to one another. Give me the number to your parole officer, and I'll handle the situation on this end. Don't ask any questions, just do what I'm requesting of you, and this will go just fine. Secondly, I'll need…"

Before she could finish, Horisha began to stand up at the table to attempt to excuse herself. Then she starts to speak.

"Listen Avery, I've just completed a 20-year bid, and I'm not in the mood to be playing games with no one that thinks they can move my mountains out my way. I know there's more than one way to climb a mountain with or without help. So thank you, but no thank you."

In that moment, Avery's inner thug came out and reached across the table and verbally snatched her soul out of her body.

"I'm trying to be nice to you and let you know that I can help you get your feet on the ground. You need to show your parole officer certain shit and I'm the woman that has all that you need at my fingertips. You need housing. I got that. You need finances. I got that too. On top of that, the 50 large that you need from my husband, I can get you more than that and send you on your way. Are you willing to listen to me, so we can both win? You need me.

Surprisingly, she sat back down, grabbed a napkin, and wrote the information down that was asked. Horisha, then, inquired to see if there was anything else Avery needed from her.

Avery looked at the paper, looked up at her, and smiled.

Avery said, "No, I'll take it from here. Thank you, that'll be all. You're free to go."

As Horisha got up from the table, she bent down and said in a sweet voice, " I caught that slick ass comment, "You're free to go." My primary language is sarcasm. Don't think you are about to own me just because you are doing me this favor. I still have your husband by the balls, and ultimately that means you as well…"

Before she could finish Avery, slid up and said, "You most certainly may have Lance by the balls, but I'm the bitch that holds the muthafucking cards. So grab his balls as hard as you want to, I won't feel shit. Have a great rest of the day sweetheart."

She winked, sat back, and finished her drink. Horisha nodded her head at me, and she parted ways.

I just stared and said, "Avery really?"

Avery responds, "Don't Avery me. How do you know her?"

"Well, technically, I don't know her. She called the office and inquired about a possible position. That's how I knew her name, and when you called it out, it shocked me because I never saw her in person. But, honestly, how many people have the name Horisha?"

"Well, you might be right, I was attempting to extend an olive branch. She was acting like she didn't need it. So, let's let the shit hit the fucking fan."

"Ok. Wait, maybe I can smooth things over, and maybe get yall on better terms, because if she gets the job at the firm, then I'll be working with her. I may even have to train her, so I don't want things to be uncomfortable."

"Sis, get your overthinking ass out of the clouds. I got this. Besides this ain't got shit to do with you. Watch me work. But I'm telling you from here on out, don't make me feel like I can't trust you. Trust is like glass, and once it's broken, you can put it back together but the remnants of the break are still obvious because. Just keep it all the way real with me, and don't think I'm threatening you; I just take my relationships seriously."

She threw a blueberry on the table to cover the drinks and said, "Come on. Let's go."

So there goes my meal, or my me time, and truth be told, they ruined my orgasm. Hell, I really didn't think that was going to go the way it went and who in the hell knew I would run into Horisha of all places in the city, the restroom of The Blue Room. So now, Avery knows all the business and more, she still never let on to me knowing what I know about Lance. But hell with what she just said to me, do I tell her what I know about Lance?

"Do you hear me talking to you? Girl, I just been running my mouth about inmate #100699. She thought she was about to dance with the verbal assassin. I think not. I just had to hand it to her politely in that restaurant and let her know."

"My fault, I was just literally recapping the moment in time."

How could all that mess happen to me in one day? Now understanding none of this has anything to do with me directly, but for whatever it's worth, Isis' name is the common denominator. That's too much for me. I gotta find Kareem and see what's up with this girl.

Pausing to think about what Avery just said I asked her, "Did you actually call her by her inmate number? Please tell me you don't know that shit. That's borderline psychotic, and I'm going to need you to seek medical attention like yesterday."

"Hell naw, I just rambled off six digits. Now you know good and well, it's going to take more than this instance to get me rattled. But on another note, before we go, I have been looking at a few places that might interest you to look at to see if you like it for the new real estate company."

"Yeah, about that, seeing we're not on the phone, you mentioned that you needed to invest in some property to make a smooth transition. Care to share now that we're face to face?"

"See it's like this, my father set up a major trust fund for the first-born grandchild before he died. That first born grandchild is Aniya, so when she graduates, she gets a nice lump sum of money. But, I need to invest it in some property, so she gets a little at a time. She definitely can't handle all that money coming to her. I have decided to take it and move it to purchase some property. I will buy her some clothes and give her a boutique. This way I can make her think she's doing something worthwhile and unbeknownst to her, it's my father's way of taking care of her from the other side."

"Oh wow, ok so I guess we couldn't have said that over the phone? Now if you want me to keep it real with you, you gotta keep it real with me."

"Ok busted. I'm getting ready to close a $5 million dollar deal with some heavy hitters and sell them one of my plugs. With the money, I have to make it look legit. That's where you come in, the bomb real estate agent. Got it?"

"Yep. I got it. So, you are the Queenpin behind all the activity going on in the city. That's why it was so easy for you to get the billboard, and you have the connection with the parole board. Hell, I know I'm missing some people, but damn. Ok and all I did was sell a measly house and this has gotten us entangled together."

"No. That's not all you did. The one thing that sold me on embarking on a friendship with you was the way you welcomed my daughter, the relationship you have with your children, and the way you carry yourself, that's real woman shit. You know, again I grew up in the house with all boys, so it's hard to trust. But, you are someone different. Furthermore, we are about to get this cake, put some cherries on top, and wash it all down with whatever type of champagne you want. My gift to you is that when our children graduate, we are on a plane to wherever. Bitch, we deserve it."

"Well, in that case, let's get this money, and tie up these loose ends."

"I'll text you the addresses of the potential places to look at for the new spot."

I smiled and responded, "Sounds good."

We hugged and parted ways.

Chapter 11

Ronnie

I need to pinch myself. This has been one hell of a day. All that extra shit that just took place and I didn't even finish my drink or get my damn fries. I really need to go home and relax. But first, I need to just take a moment and regroup. Why haven't I heard from Kareem all day? That's not like him, but as he always says, as I attempt to mock him.

"Don't worry about me. If something happens to me, trust me there's people that know how to get in contact with you so you'll know what to do next."

Yeah, well that's all fine and good, but where is this nigga at?

Driving home, my mind is racing a thousand miles a minute and literally I just want to get home. This time get me a glass of wine, take a hot bath, and do absolutely nothing. I need a mental break from society.

Turning onto the cul-de-sac, I see those two black SUVs on post to make sure I'm good. Since they're here, I know Kareem ain't too far away. But, I still haven't heard from him. Luckily for me, my house looks quiet and that means there's no one in there and I can go and relax.

Whew! Let me pour myself a glass of wine. Lately, I've been on a red wine kick. I found a local wine called "Sweet Revenge" and oh my goodness it is amazing. Ahhh, a moment of pure quietness, no children, no television, no phone, no nothing, and I can't believe the day I had. As I am sitting relaxing, I swear I could just doze off, but I need to get dinner for the boys and make sure they're taken care of before I just go ahead and fall out. The moment I begin to sip my wine, I hear the most horrible sound that completely interrupts my mode. It's my cell phone vibrating. I really got to get it because there could be a few people that may need me. Racing back to the foyer to grab my purse, I think I hear voices.

"Hello, Isis speaking."

"Boss lady, they are trying to put me in jail. This hoe ass nigga told them I jumped on him and he already been down here. Come down to the 32nd Precinct and straighten all this out please."

Baffled by what Ronnie just told me on the phone, I swear I hear voices.

"Ok, Ronnie. Here I come. Give me a few moments to get out of the house and I'm on my way."

As I'm ending my phone call, I open up the door to wave in the men in black. At this rate, I don't want to get caught slipping and end up hurting someone or being hurt.

"How can I help you, Isis?"

"I just got home and I know I'm extremely tired, but I swear I hear voices in the upstairs portion of the house and with all the stuff going on, I just figured I'd have yall check it out."

"No problem. Kareem told us to assist you in any way you needed help. Now, is there supposed to be anyone else here?"

"I have 2 children, but I didn't see the car. So, I can't say they're not here, but usually they would be in the kitchen."

"Wait outside while we check it out."

Stepping outside, I had to have a quick talk with my angel, my Granny.

"Hey beautiful, I know you may be cursing me out because of all the stuff you see going on, but I really want to tell you I'm not at fault. This is crazy, but you know the universe is showing out.

As I'm reflecting with my ancestors, one of the men in black approaches me and says "Ma'am we found the problem, it was the PS 5. Those games have live interactive voice controls. Apparently, whoever played it last, didn't turn it off, so you were right, you did hear voices. Thankfully, nothing to worry about."

"That damned Dino, I'm fighting him once I get back home. That shit damned near gave me a heart attack."

Well, now that the coast is clear, let me take my ass down to this police station, so I can get Ronnie's ass out of holding. On my way down, let me call Avery, since she has so many connections. I hope she can assist me with this. On second thought, I'd rather not. She is the queen pin and no one needs to see her coming out of the police station whether it's good, bad, or indifferent. Good thing the station is only about 15 minutes away from my house. That'll give me time to mentally prepare this lie I'm getting ready to tell, so we can get Ronnie out of holding.

Finally making it to the precinct, I'm not sure what happened between the phone call and the drive over, but Ronnie was walking out the precinct. As he makes his way over to my vehicle, we have a small exchange.

"Boss Lady, that nigga, De'Angelo, got me fucked up. He must have come down here to make a report after he was escorted out the building by security. He made claims that I jumped on him. He even said I invited him up to the office to see him, I'm so over all the goddamned lies. The only things that saved me was my telling them to call security and the fact that I just left the urgent care. I was able to show them my discharge papers. It was a clear indication that he was the assailant and not the victim. I swear I'm putting a hit out on his bitch ass."

We both laughed in unison.

"Well, Ronnie, you know we gotta switch some stuff up because we're dealing with a real-life maniac. I can't wait to see what tricks he thinks he has up his sleeve for me. Go ahead and get yourself together and if you're feeling up to it, then I'll see you tomorrow. Is that cool?"

Ronnie says, "Yeah, I'm going to head home and get some much needed rest. I have to get my strength up because we moving on up like the Jeffersons to that deluxe penthouse office in the sky."

"Boy, get yo' ass in the car and call me, if you need me."

KeanaMonique

Chapter 12

Isis

That's it. I'm going back home, and turning this phone off. No text, no incoming or outgoing phone calls period. Today has been completely insane. I can't even begin to wrap my mind around all the things that have happened in this small time period. Sadly, it's not even late yet. I, honestly, don't care to see anyone other than my children. I don't want to hear anyone else's drama.

Driving from the police station back home only gave me a few moments to clear my head before I made it home. Hopefully, my boys are there. The first thing I'm gonna do is knock Dino in between the stove and the refrigerator for leaving that damn game on. That shit almost made me have a heart attack. Then to think, I had to have those stupid guards come in and check it out. I don't know if I'm being paranoid or a punk bitch. Normally that shit wouldn't have bothered me, but for whatever reason it's troublesome. I know I just gotta go in here and burn my sage, open some windows, cleanse my dwelling and my aura, take a relaxing bath, and start over tomorrow.

Pulling up at home, a weird feeling just came over me. As I'm grabbing my purse and keys, I'm paying extra attention to my surroundings. The men in black are still here. The neighborhood appears to be quiet as always. Hopefully, my children are inside and they are good, because this feeling is uncomfortable. Universe please, I'm totally drained. I can't take any more surprises.

"Hey, Momma!" Dino says as he comes running up to greet me.

No matter how mad I may be, when he greets me this way, it's just an overwhelming expression of love. It just makes me melt.

"Hey buddy, you know you scared momma earlier today. You left that PS5 on and whoever you were playing the game with today was trying to reach you and all I heard was voices. It scared me half to death. Just remember to turn it off when you're finished, please."

"Mommy, I always turn my game off when I'm done playing it, just for that very reason."

"Well, Dino, if you turned it off, then why was it on? That makes no sense. Just remember to turn it off when you finish playing with it."

"Ok, Mommy, but I always turn it off."

"Don't go back and forth with me. Just do like I asked you to do."

Now, normally, he wouldn't argue with me about anything, but in this case, he's adamant about the fact that he turned it off. If I let my mind wander, then I know damned well this muthafucka ain't been in my house trying to send no fucking messages. Let me find out he's on some bullshit. This is the last stop he'll make before he visits the upper room.

"Ryan, what are you doing? What are we eating? Please tell me you got dinner under control, because after the day I've had, I'm exhausted."

"Momma, what do you feel like eating? I can cook or I can order something. But, you still have the leftovers from the Mediterranean food Kareem brought here."

"If I eat that, then what will y'all eat on?"

"I can cook some spaghetti. It's quick and simple and I know Dino will be alright with that. Besides, we can have the rest for tomorrow, if I cook more than enough. Dang, Momma, you look like you're tired. Was your day long? Did you have to go show some new houses?"

At that moment, I knew I forgot to follow up with Melinda Jacobs about the open houses for the new showings. Damn, I can never get enough rest or not think about the office for 5 minutes. I'm home now. She's probably gone too. It's just going to have to wait until tomorrow.

"Alexa, remind me to call Melinda Jacobs in the morning."

"Ryan, I'm headed up to take a shower. I'll be back and we can all have dinner together when I get out."

"Alright, Moms, take your time. I still gotta cook the spaghetti, but I got you."

Making my way upstairs, I checked my phone for the last time before I silenced my ringer. I can't turn it off, as bad as I want to, but I'll just turn the ringer off, so I can see and return all my missed calls, if any.

Before I forget, let me get all my belongings together, so when I get out of the shower I can just get dressed in the bathroom. There's nothing more I hate than to leave the warm steamy bathroom and walk into a cold room. It totally ruins my experience. As a matter of fact, if Ryan has to cook, then there's no need for me to shower, I can take a hot ass bubble bath and relax. Making my way to the bathroom with the change of bathing plans, I detour back downstairs to get my wine from earlier along with the bottle. It's been one of those days.

Preparing my bath, I have my bath salts, rose petals, rose oil, candles, and my music playing softly. This water is about to give me life. Taking off all my clothes, one item at a time, just made me feel like I was taking a thousand pounds of weight off my body. I just want to sit in the bathtub, relax, sip my wine in total silence, and have a serene moment just for me. I give everything to everybody and I hardly take time to recharge my personal battery.

Well, tonight it is. My children are home doing whatever it is they do, and I'm here wondering who the fuck turned that damn game on? But for now, even that thought has to get pushed to the back of the line, because it's not important. Come to think of it, I still haven't heard from Kareem.

This is so not like him. But hell, even he was going to have to take a seat in the back of the bus. This trip is for Isis "Muthafucking" Carrington. I couldn't help but laugh at that shit. I swear I would've loved to see his face when I said it to De'Angelo over the phone.

Chapter 13

The Mall

Waking up refreshed, relaxed, and rejuvenated, but I still can't figure out why I haven't heard from Kareem. This is so unlike him. He better have a damn good reason why he hasn't called me back, and if Mya has had those punk ass minions do something to him, I swear I'll blow this muthafucking city to pieces.

There's so much to do and so little time, I need to check on Ronnie to make sure he's alright to come to work today, I need to call Avery to see what's good with the Lance situation, then call this low-down ass nigga, Lance, to see what the fuck he done got into. Finally, I need to contact the precinct to see what detective is in charge of this case, so I can see how to handle this scandal. I'm definitely going to show this nigga, De'Angelo, who the fuck I am, because clearly, he hasn't figured it out yet. Nevertheless, let me get my day started.

Jumped out the shower feeling fresh to death, grabbed me something simple to wear. I grab some True Religion skinny jeans, a cute top, these Louboutins, and a blazer. Of course, let me put my tennis shoes in the back of my car in case I need to get it in. Laughing to myself, that sounded so 'hood. I know good and damn well I ain't fighting anybody, but this little piece Kareem got me is going with me everywhere. If something happens and I don't have it on me, then he is going to be tripping.

As I leave the house, I leave a note for my children and let them know what's going down when I come home tonight. Shaking my head, those watchers are still posted. I wonder if they heard from Kareem. I know if something has happened to him, he already told me that there's people on standby to let me know what's good. So far no one has called, so everything has to be alright, but it doesn't stop me from worrying.

Now that I'm in the mobile office, let me contact Ronnie, to see how he's doing. As I pick up my phone to call, it starts ringing through the car.

"Isis speaking."

"Boss lady, um we got a problem, here at the office, they are telling me the suite ain't ready and we can't come to work today. It won't be ready 'til tomorrow 'cause they gotta paint it, put our stuff in, and set up everything."

"Well, what can I do about it? Meet me downstairs. We'll meet up and discuss other business. Are you down for some retail therapy?"

"Um, hell yeah, if you buying, then I know I can use it. But, let's only do budget shopping. I'll show you how I catch all these deals."

"Anything for you. Don't think you are getting this treatment often. I'm only being this generous because you've been traumatized. Are the phone lines working?"

"You know what, Boss, I don't know if they've been transferred yet."

"Well, find out and transfer them to your cell phone, so the potential clients can still have access to us, if need be. I'll be downstairs waiting when you finish."

Well ,what the entire fuck? I got cute to prance around the mall. Well, not in these shoes, see I knew I was prepared when I grabbed tennis shoes and put them in the back of the car. Hell, who knows what may happen hanging out with Ronnie? While I have a few moments, let me shoot Avery a text and see if she's cool, and also check in with her about this prom situation because I swear Ryan doesn't tell me anything. As I'm typing the text message, my favorite song, *Loving You,* by Minnie Ripperton comes through the speakers. Just as I start to belt out the la la la la la la's, Ronnie interrupts and finishes it with the most beautiful version of that song.

Snapping me out of my slight trance, "Well damn, song bird, that sounded pretty good, for a man."

In an extremely manly voice, he says "Thank you."

We both burst out laughing.

"Get in the car, so we can go grab breakfast and hit the mall. Then, you can show me how to budget shop. By the way, do you happen to have your case number on you? So, I can call and check to see what detectives have been assigned to your case."

"I most certainly do." as he buckles his seat belt.

"I got the calls transferred to my cell phone, and I took the liberty of getting the messages off the voicemail. Boss lady, what's up with Horisha? She called again. Did you ever figure out what she wanted?"

"Oh yeah, she actually just passed the real estate exam and she's looking for employment. Honestly, I think her interview with Mr. Donahue and I was scheduled for today. I'll have to call her back to reschedule."

But first, we're headed to grab some breakfast, before the mall opens, and then we'll walk and handle business.

My mobile office plans have changed, since I have a passenger. Before leaving the office, I sent a few text messages; one to Avery, the next to Horisha, then finally, against my better judgment, Lance. I swear I don't know what type of street drug he's on but clearly, it's gotta be some good stuff for him to think he can confide in me without me spilling my beans to Avery. Thinking of Avery, I gotta make sure she's serious about the office building. No need to get my hopes high and nothing happens. As I'm driving, I see Ronnie snap his fingers in front of my face.

"Boss Lady, where did you just mentally travel off to? I've been calling your name and trying to let you know about some office stuff, but clearly you aren't on this planet."

Laughing slightly, "Boy, please you know I'm the queen of multitasking, so don't get it twisted. I actually heard everything you said, which by the way, wasn't much."

"Humor me", he replied.

"Well before we left the office, you reminded me for a second time that you transferred all the office calls to your cell phone. You also mentioned the internet flier needs to be approved before we go forward with the promotion, and lastly, you told me that I need to increase your pay, due to you being assaulted on the job."

Looking speechless, Ronnie replied, "Well damn, I guess yo' wanna be ratchet self was paying attention. Excuse me."

Still no calls or return text messages, so as we were pulling up to the mall, I valet it because I don't want to deal with parking and walking.

"Boss Lady, first stop, we gotta go by Auntie Annie's, so I can get a cinnamon pretzel with a side of cream cheese since you rode past every place that sold breakfast."

"Ronnie, my apologies, anyway, what do you know about those pretzels? Those saved me all through high school. I can do you one better and tell you I used to work there for one of my first jobs. I haven't always been in real estate."

We both laughed as we made our way to our first stop.

Once we got the pretzel, we toasted our lemonade and we were well on our way.

As Ronnie is showing me how he shops, I hear someone call my name. Now, I know I'm 'hood famous, but not enough for people to be calling my name in the mall so early in the morning. These are work hours and people should be working. I hear it again. It's a female voice, but not familiar enough that I can recognize it immediately. So, I stopped to do a slight turn and who do I see fast pacing towards me with a young man walking behind her, none other than Horisha.

Chapter 14

The Mall

"Good morning Isis, how are you?" Horisha says.

"I'm well, thank you. And yourself?"

Horisha hesitated as she asked her next question.

"Excuse me for asking, but don't I have an interview with you and Mr. Donahue this afternoon, around 2:00 right?"

"Well actually, the interview may or may not still be going on, we've had some interior glitches that need to be handled. They should be finished by this afternoon, but I'll let you know in time enough to get yourself together."

"Sounds good," Horisha replied. "I'm sorry, please forgive my rudeness, this is my son, Strickland. He's my grown man. He's taking me shopping, so I can get ready for this interview. Strickland, this is Ms. Carrington. She works for the real estate company I have an interview with this afternoon."

As I look over to him, he looks extremely familiar, but I can't put my finger on it. His eyebrows are super thick, his skin is soft like dark milk chocolate, his waves are on swim, and his eyes, one of them are brown, and the other is black. Now that's a unique trait to have. Maybe he has one from each parent, but oh well. His teeth are sparkling, crooked in a cute way, but clean. Well groomed and his mannerisms resemble that of someone who was raised by older individuals but who am I, so much for an initial assessment.

As I leaned over to shake his hand and introduce them to Ronnie, He beat me to it.

"Hi, I'm Ronnie, her lovely assistant. I'm the ying to her yang, the up to her down, the left to her right, the..."

As I interrupted, I'm sure they got the picture. As the three of them exchanged pleasantries, this eerie feeling crept up on me and I couldn't shake it. Alright universe what am I supposed to be seeing at this moment. You always come through and show me what I need to see.

"It was great meeting you, Strickland".

"It was my pleasure as well, Ms. Carrington and nice meeting you also Ronnie."

"Horisha, I'll have Ronnie send you the information about the interview this afternoon, whether it's a go or reschedule."

"Thank you, I look forward to hearing from you later."

As we all parted ways, I needed to shake this eerie feeling. As I looked over to Ronnie, to attempt to explain the feeling, it's almost as if we were in sync.

He turned and said, "Boss Lady, is it me or did you get a fucked-up feeling meeting the two of them?"

"I wouldn't call it a fucked up feeling, but there was definitely something in the air. We'll figure that out later and now it's time for you to show me how to shop on a budget, the Ronnie way."

Walking and talking in the mall, we seemed as if we had been friends forever, and it's almost as if we could've been mother and son, however it was nice to just kick it. In and out of stores, he's actually giving me tips on how to shop on a budget, now quite frankly I know what it's like to budget shop, but it's always nice to see someone else's point of view.

In the midst of shopping, and lollygagging through the mall, I think I see Jaylen, and in fact, yes it was him.

Walking up to us, Ronnie nudges me and says, “Boss, ain't that the dude from the wedding?”

“Yeah, that’s Jaylen, De’Angelo’s nephew.”

Jaylen walked up and greeted us both.

Then he leans in for a hug and whispers in my ear, “Meet me on the opposite side of the food court. You know where the family restrooms are, so I can give you this dick.”

As enticing as that sounds, I’m here with Ronnie, and I am unsure on how to shake him.

I reply back, “Give me 10 minutes and I’ll be in there.”

Jaylen walks away

Ronnie says, “Didn’t you say that’s De’Angelo nephew?”

I simply reply, “Indeed, he is.”

As Ronnie starts talking, in my brain, I’m calculating when to dip off and go get my back blown out. Right now, I’m unsure if he can, because last time I took advantage of the situation we were on

Belle Isle, and I got what I needed and left. So, I guess I owe him a second chance to see exactly what he is working with. No, it's not like I'm truly going to entertain the thought of having something serious with him. It's just sex. And right now, I'm in need of getting fucked really good. Now, let's see if he can pull it off.

"Ronnie, I'm getting ready to go to the bathroom, you good?

"Yeah, Boss Lady, I'm about to go to a few stores and see what I can find, gone head and handle your business, and we'll meet up. Just call the phone when you get done. I mean dang, it shouldn't take you that long to pee, but you know how y'all geriatric people do."

Laughing together, I nodded, and headed to the mission spot, aka, the bathroom.

Now normally, I wouldn't pay him any attention, but for whatever reason his authority piqued my interest and I needed to get the release I was looking for. As I made my way to the family restroom, I couldn't help but walk with anticipation, because if I recall correctly his slong was a pretty decent size and extremely workable.

Approaching the family restroom, I really had to think if it was worth it or not, then I mean Kareem was still missing in action. Furthermore, this is De'Angelo's nephew. I don't know if he's doing some pay back stuff for his uncle or is this just something he wants to do? Afterall, he did tell me to hit him up when we last saw each other at the wedding.

As the nerves began to dissipate, I walked into the family restroom to find the lights out, "Jaylen" I called out.

There was no answer and out of the darkness a hand wrapped around my waist, and one around the back of my neck.

Then, I heard a voice say to me, "So, you just fuck me on Belle Isle and then ghost me like I never existed? You owe me. Now, let me see what that mouth do."

All of a sudden, I heard the door lock and he turned me around and tried to take control of the situation, but to his surprise, aint' no hoe in Isis Carrington. I quickly reversed the situation and took control. I took one hand and grabbed his throat and with the other hand I grabbed his package.

I placed my mouth against his ear and whispered to him, "I'm Isis Muthafuckin' Carrington, now you show me what that mouth do."

Before I knew it, he had unbuckled my pants and lifted me up on the sink of the restroom and slid my panties to the side and inserted his tongue into my juice box as if he was sliding his erect penis inside me. I must admit it felt so good to have his tongue gliding up and down my precious pearl.

Moaning in pleasure, he inserted a finger inside to enhance the experience. Trying to think back to the Belle Isle incident I couldn't recall if he had taken the time to taste my love below, but it didn't really matter at this point because he was devouring it as if it was a delicacy that he had been longing to eat. Surprisingly, he's actually great in the oral department, which kinda makes me wonder why I really ghosted him to begin with.

I had had enough, my internal cavity needed to be stabbed with just the right amount of force and I honestly don't know if he can do it. I was on top last time.

Slightly giggling to myself I said, "Fuck this pussy."

Jaylen replied, "I thought you'd never ask."

Thumbing through his pocket to find his condom, he still has a mouth full of me and once he located the condom, I heard him rip the wrapper, then the rest was history. He picked me up and bent me over. All I had to grab was my ankles to get a balanced stance, as I was preparing myself for entry, it slid in and I couldn't believe what he was working with.

Moaning in unexpected bliss, this was just what my body needed. It was just the right length and the right circumference to fill my pleasure palace just right. As he's going deeper and deeper inside, I can hear him as he's trying to be all manly, but he can't help to verbally express himself.

"Damn, Isis, this pussy is so wet. Shit, you about to make me cum."

As he's talking, I bent my knees a little bit and repositioned myself and grabbed the handicapped bar and began to throw it back like only I can. I swear I was giving it up so good I was about make my own self cum. As I'm giving up the ass, he throws the dick my way and before you know it we're both moaning in pleasure as we both get ready to reach the finish line at the same time.

It's happening, in between breaths I say, "I'm cuming. Stay right there. Yes, baby boy, stay right there. Ahh! Yes, here it cums!"

I can hear him also, telling me to let it go.

He says, "Shit, baby throw it back. I'm about to buss."

As he's gripping my hips, his stroke changes, and he starts moving faster from side to side. Both of us moaning in unison, we both reach the level of perfection at the same time. As his strokes get slower, but yet still very much hard and firm, I attempt to slide away from him. He continues to thrust in and out and it's feeling amazing. When he finally does finish the last glide, he pulls out, bends down on his knees, and finishes the job. Eating it from the back. As he's sucking the life out of my pleasure palace, my legs start shaking and I almost want to have another orgasm, but I'll refrain and not give up too much too quickly. As he gave her a final kiss, it was soft and sweet. He tickled the tip of my clitoris just right.

He backed away from me, to assist me up. Once I was in the upright position, we locked eyes and for a moment a feeling came over me like damn.

He broke the trance by touching my lips with his fingers and saying the words "Did I satisfy you?"

Not wanting to be overly eager to answer the question, I replied and stated, "It was a start."

I gathered my belongings, did a quick wipe up, gave myself one last mirror check, and proceeded to find Ronnie. Exiting the restroom, he told me to hit him later.

I replied and said, "I don't have the number. Google the office and ask for me."

Observing my surroundings in the food court, I didn't really see anyone that I would know or that would focus on the fact that someone else would be coming out of the same restroom as me. So, I shook my hair, fixed my clothes, and went to find Ronnie.

Walking through the food court, I can't seem to locate him, as if he would be standing in a certain location. So, I did what I should've done in the first place, shoot a text message.

As I'm waiting for a reply, I swing by a kiosk to check my look, and before I could check myself, I hear his voice, "Aye Boss Lady, I'm over here."

Taking a deep breath and gaining my composure, I walk over to him. He's standing there talking to none other than Ms. Kupenda, herself. Talking to myself, I'm wondering like damn why do I keep running into this chick? I mean is the universe trying to tell me something? Approaching the two of them, I made my presence known and surprisingly she was cordial and she spoke in return. Now damn it, my chance to be a bitch is out the window. I guess that's alright, after all I did tell Ronnie that I would work on not being so rude every time I saw her. Since I just got broke off in the bathroom, I'm on ice mode. So, I honestly don't think there's anything that she can say to me to alter me, I'm feeling damn good.

"Ronnie, I'll be over here waiting for the two of you to finish your conversation."

"Alright Boss, I'll be right there."

Once they wrapped it up, they embraced and parted ways. Oddly enough, Kupenda even said bye to me and wished me a great afternoon. Now I'm really like what the fuck?

Walking through the mall, Ronnie notices something, then he turns to me and says "Um, Boss lady are you alright?"

"Yes certainly, why do you ask?"

"Because you look like you just got finished, and he took a deep breath, Boss Lady you didn't?"

"Didn't what? I truly have no idea what you're talking about."

"Oh hell naw, you gave it up in the bathroom?"

"Ronnie, I did no such thing. Why would you even think I would do such a thing in a public place?"

"I know that look, and you are giving me toilet sex vibes."

Bursting out in tears from laughter, I couldn't confess. I had to continue to act as if I didn't know what he was talking about. As hard as it was, I don't think I'm doing a pretty good job at it, because he is head strung on telling me I had toilet sex in the mall.

"Ronnie, please let it go. You truly are wrong. I didn't do anything other than go to the ladies' room."

"Yeah, ok, I'll let it go this time, but pardon me and I'll say this and then I'll drop it. Now, that was Jaylen who walked up to you and then all of a sudden you had to go to the ladies' room. Well, that is De'Angelo's nephew and if he is well endowed in that department like his uncle is, then I would've had me some toilet dick too."

Looking over at him, giving him the side eye, before I could state my thoughts, my cell phone rang.

"Isis Carrington speaking. Oh ok, yes we're just at the mall. I'll confirm with her and we'll be right in. Is the office ready yet? Great, Ronnie is with me and we'll be right there. It's still set for 2pm this afternoon. Perfect, see you shortly. Thank you, Mr. Donahue."

Saved by the bell, looking over at Ronnie, I politely and sarcastically say to him, "Let's go. The office is ready. Contact Horisha to confirm for 2pm. Let's get back to the office."

Frozen in mid step, he clears his throat and says, "Don't think this conversation is over with, Ms. Toilet Time Tina."

Laughing hysterically, I continued to walk and let him catch up. There's no way I'm confirming or denying these true allegations.

As I strut my toilet-sex-having ass around the mall, I can't help but wonder where the fuck Kareem is. This is really starting to irritate me. He's never gone this long without checking in and quite frankly I think he's outta town, but I can't be sure without validation. Damn, I wish I knew where this hoe Mya lived because I would do a random drive by or check out the scenery at least.

As we are making our way out the mall, Ronnie finally catches up to me and says, "You don't gotta tell me the truth, but I already know what you did. Trust me Triple T, I mean Boss Lady, every girl has to have at least one secret."

Continuing to walk out the mall, I replied with a sinister grin, "You're right, but I'll never tell."

Chapter 15

Horisha

Walking into the office, Ronnie and I were greeted by security. Now that's a new routine, but I guess now you can't be too safe, considering what took place with Ronnie and De'Angelo. I'm still amazed at how De'Angelo got past security in the first place. As we're standing in the foyer building, we were asked to turn in our physical keys, so we could receive our scannable cards that get us in the building and on to the top floor. The top floor is where our new penthouse suite is located, of course.

Once we've been scanned in and have our cards in our hands, we're off to see our new office. Working at Keys Realty is a great place to work, I mean, the perks, the days off, and the bonuses are always a plus. However, I hate that they're going through all this trouble for me. I just have to solidify a few things on my end and I can get the fuck on to bigger and better things. Speaking of things, I really need to chop it up with Avery. She hasn't called me back all day. Although it's only the first half of the day, I'm really starting to think she and Kareem are magicians because both of them have some strong disappearing skills.

As we make it to the top floor, the view is spectacular. The entire room is glass and since it's so high up there is no need for blinds or any type of window treatments. The skyline of the city is breathtaking. I mean who wouldn't want to get bent over the desk and have an orgasm just looking at this view.

Breaking my daydream, Ronnie yells out, "Boss Lady, it's almost time for the interview. Do you need me to accompany you to take notes? Will you and Mr. Donahue be alright?"

Thinking to myself, now when has he sat in on interviews? He has to be up to something, or he knows something I don't. Being careful not to yell too loud, I'm unsure if these walls are soundproof, so I have to use my inside voice.

"Ronnie, come here for a sec please. Riddle me this, since when do you sit in on interviews? Is there something you know that I don't? Is there something I need to know and you're not telling me?"

Giving me the look as only he can, he responds and says "No, it ain't like that I just wanna be nosy to see if she discloses why she went to prison, and if what the word on the street is true or not."

Looking a bit confused, I say, "Excuse me, what exactly are the streets saying and why is it any of your concern?"

"Well, you know Boss Lady, any associate here is my concern. Besides, I don't want anything out there to compromise anyone's security here, especially when my security has already been compromised."

Well since he put it that way, I guess I gotta believe him. After all, Ronnie did just get assaulted and I guess he is a little apprehensive about all the new employees. However, he doesn't get to sit in on this interview, and besides it's confidential anyway.

"Thank you, but no thank you. I appreciate the gesture, but Mr. Donahue and I can handle it. But when she gets here, send her into my office and we'll both go to Mr. Donahue's office together."

As he exits my office, I can't help but to marvel at the look of this office. I guess I can see why they call it the penthouse suite. There's a whole studio apartment in the corner of this office. I guess I don't have to go home, if I'm having a late day at the office. Hell that wouldn't be me, I'm always taking my ass home to my boys. But hey, it's here for a reason. Nevertheless, it's decorated amazingly. I can't help but to wonder why Mr. Donahue was so gracious to offer this to Ronnie and I. I mean his office isn't even this nice. I swear something in the milk ain't clean. Mr. D is up to something, and I'm going to find out just what it is.

As he leans in the doorway of my office, he snaps his fingers and says, "Boss Lady, Horisha is here to see you. Should I send her in?"

"Sure. Give me a few seconds. Let me contact Mr. Donahue and let him know we're on our way down."

When I lean over to grab my cell phone to shoot Mr. Donahue a text, my phone rings and it's Avery.

"Hey girl, is everything ok?"

I immediately say when I answer the phone.

"Girl, yeah, just leaving the bank and gotta do some running around before Aniya gets outta school. You good?" Avery asks.

"Oh yeah, I'm good. I'm just getting ready to interview Horisha. You remember she applied to be a real estate agent here, so I'm going to try to be as professional as I can. I need to get this tea as to why she really went to prison or to see if what you said is true? And why would she apply to this office, out of all the offices in the Metro-Detroit area?"

Avery responds eagerly, "Now, you're speaking my language. Find out what you can and let me know. Oh yeah, I think I just found the perfect spot for your new real estate office. So, call me back when you get a moment."

The call was disconnected. Laughing to myself, she never says bye. She just hangs up. I guess it's something to get used to.

Finally being able to send that text to let him know we're on our way down, I walk out and see Horisha sitting with Ronnie exchanging pleasantries about God knows what. Whatever it is, I'm sure he's taking all the notes he needs for whatever security agenda he may have.

"Hi, Horisha, follow me, please. We will head down a few floors to Mr. Donahue's office. You look nervous. Are you ok?'

Shakingly, she responds, "I'm a bit nervous. This is actually the first interview I've been on since I've been released from prison. I know it's all in my head, but I really just want to do well in this interview, secure the job, and start being a productive citizen out here. Also, so my damn parole officer can get off my back."

"I get that. Well, no worries. You'll do fine, if you start to get nervous just tap your foot 3 times and I'll chime in and reroute the interview. Does that sound like a plan?"

"Yes, that sounds great. Thank you so much."

I respond with a smile and say, "In that case, let's go secure the job."

As we enter into Mr. Donahue's office, he's sitting behind his desk trying to look as if he's working.

"Good afternoon, Mr. Donahue, this is Horisha. She is the new applicant that applied for the realtor position that was posted on a few employment sites."

With a large unsuspecting smile, he replied, "Yes, Horisha, I've actually been going over your resume and background check."

Mr. Donahue pauses and chooses his words carefully, "I see you took the exam while you were in a federal institution? I just have one question for you. Your answer will be the determining factor, if you get the job or not. We sell houses, Horisha. Do you plan on hiding any drug paraphernalia in any of the houses?"

I blink rapidly three times, because I'm hoping they can't see that my eyes are about to pop out of my head. Like, what does he expect her to say? 'Yes, I plan on hiding drugs in the houses.' I continue to watch his line of questioning.

Mr. Donahue continues, "Now, if you plan on that, then I don't want you working here. To be honest, you're already a flight risk and to take you on is a risk in itself. But, Isis vouched for you, so I'm giving you this opportunity. It may seem silly, but again I'm asking you, do I have to worry about that funny business?"

He pulled his glasses down and waited for her response. As we agreed on her to tap her foot three times, in case she got nervous, I looked down and her foot was tapping away at this point.

But before I could intervene, she jumped right in and said, "Mr. Donahue, sir, let's get one thing clear, I have not now, nor ever sold or hid any type of drugs. My stint in prison was due to someone else's failure to take responsibility. Since I'm no snitch, I did the time without ever doing the crime. So, if you want me to honestly represent your company and sell houses, then you need to look no further. However, if you think for one second that I'm going to be the butt of anyone's jokes about my past life and choices I've made, then I don't think Keys Realty is for me. With all due respect, I thank you for your time. I'll completely understand, if you choose not to hire me."

She stood up like a boss and proceeded to walk out the office. When I came out of the initial shock of what just happened, I told her to wait outside for me.

"Mr. Donahue, did you really just say that to her?"

"I, most certainly, did. She needs to have tough skin if she wants to work in this field. Honestly, she reminds me so much of you. Since she does, you have full responsibility to groom her, find her an assistant, and you can train her. Ronnie can train the assistant. Tell her, she's hired."

"Oh my goodness, thank you so much. I know she was nervous to do the interview with you, but you can rest assured that I'll have her groomed in no time, thank you."

"Anytime," he replied, "and one more thing before you go. I'm telling you first, but I'll be retiring. I have been thinking about this for some time now. After careful consideration, I have decided that I want you to take over the firm."

"Mr. Donahue, I'm speechless and as much as I want to take it over, my dream was to always have my own firm."

"Well, what do you need to make it your own? I've given you the penthouse suite. I'm increasing your commission. I'm ultimately letting you groom your own staff. What else do you need? You're the only one here that I fully trust to leave my business to. Don't answer now, just think about it and let me know by the end of the week."

Shocked and flabbergasted, I say, "Thank you again, I'll let you know.

Exiting his office, I see Horisha down the hallway pacing back and forth. Trying to keep a straight face as I walked up to her was hard, but I did my best.

"Well, you made one hell of an impression."

But before I could finish, she interrupted me by saying, "I fucked up. Didn't I?"

Laughing slightly, I just shook my head and said, "No, baby girl, you got the position and the fact that you said what you said, he said you reminded him of me. So that was the attitude that got you hired, and I have to train you. We'll get you an assistant, and you'll have everything you need to get started by the beginning of next week."

She was so happy. She let out a little scream and she immediately hugged me.

"Thank you so much for helping me out with this interview,"

"Trust me, I didn't do anything. That was all you."

As Horisha begins to walk toward the elevator, she starts talking to herself.

Horisha talking to herself and feeling so accomplished, makes me smile.

Then, I hear her say, "Ok, job security? Check that off the list. Next thing I need to handle is telling Lance."

While she is scrolling through her phone, I walk up and push the button for the elevator.

I say to her, "I'm sorry, but did you just say '...telling Lance'? I'm not trying to pry, but why would you tell him you obtained employment?"

"Oh, girl please, I ain't telling that nigga shit about me. The only thing I need to tell that hoe ass nigga is the secret I've been holding for almost 20 years."

Now, I'm afraid to ask, but I just gotta know. My conscience won't let me be great, if I don't inquire.

Jokingly, I say, "What secret? Spill the tea. Are you his long-lost baby momma?"

Before I could actually get the joke out of my mouth, she answered.

Horisha said, "Yeah. I had the baby while I was in prison. He was raised by my mother who can't stand him. So yeah, to answer your question. Yes, my son is his and no he doesn't know. I'd like to keep it that way until I tell him myself."

"Oh, shit your secret is safe with me. Those aren't my beans to spill, so you can have at it."

During that awkward moment of silence, it was interrupted by the elevator door opening for us to depart.

She stepped in and said, "Are you getting on?"

Still stuck in disbelief, I told her I needed to go get some paperwork from human resources to have her fill out. As we locked eyes, she did the hush sign and the doors closed.

Chapter 16

The Office

Talking to myself , and as I replay everything that just went down, I think I just put my foot in my mouth. But, seriously, I was only joking with her. I swear I don't want this to backfire on me and have this whole ordeal blow up in my face. But then again, I really didn't do anything. I only made a joke, which in fact turned out to be true. Alright now, Isis, you're rambling. This truly has nothing to do with you and you have to keep it strictly professional. You have to stay in your lane and most importantly, you have to make the next move your best move. Now, it's time to move these chess pieces. I think I know exactly what piece to put in rotation.

Now, Mr. Donahue just threw me for a total loop. Who would've thought that he was considering retirement and passing the entire firm to the only black woman working here? Not to mention, I am the youngest. I swear I gotta pat myself on the back. I know I am killing it around here.

I say to myself, "Now look, Isis, don't go getting the big head. You have to crunch some numbers before you just commit to this type of position."

In times like these I swear I need to hear from Kareem. He'd know exactly what to say to help me make this move. I have a few more days before I have to give an answer, so hopefully he resurfaces. Then, he and I can go over this stuff.

With all this going on, I clearly walked right past HR and straight up the stairs to the office.

Entering the office with the key card is pretty dope, if I do say so myself. I don't even have to show it to anyone. The fact that it opens the door when it's in a certain range is enough for me because it's all about safety.

"Ronnie, I need you in my office right now. As a matter of fact, I need you to beat me there. I need you to grab your notebook, and a pencil, or whatever you decide to write with, but just know it's about to get hectic over the next few weeks."

"Boss Lady, oh my goodness, is everything alright? I can't take all this pressure. What's about to go down? Did she mess up in the interview? Did it all go to hell in a handbasket? I mean, come on, spill it. What happened up there? I know you got something, 'cause I'm prepared for note taking."

Before he could ask another question, I just shut it down. I told him let's get to business.

"Listen, there's a time to play and a time to work. Right now, it's work time. So, I need you to contact HR and get the new employee handbook. Then, get everything set for Horisha to move into the office we just transferred from. Next, Have security get some different keys cut to that office, or just inquire to see how much it'll be to have a touchless entry like ours. Also, go get your training manuals and get ready to train a new assistant."

"Ok, I think I've got everything. But wait, who am I training?"

Looking up at him with a soft but stern look that said, "Don't ask me another question."

All I could say was one name, "Kupenda."

I continued on, "Now, enough with the questions already. I'll give you answers when it's the right time, but now we're in work mode. I need you to put these ducks in a row. Oh, and before you leave, get Kupenda on line 4. Transfer it when she answers. Before you ask, you better not even think about listening in on the conversation, I'm sure she'll tell you what you need to know, if it all goes well."

With a slight look of somewhat disappointment, he grabbed his notebook, pen, and his hurt little feelings. He sashayed his pretty little self-back to the front office and got Kupenda on the line. Once I heard him confirm it was her, I put my game face on and promised myself not to cut up on her.

KeanaMonique

"Boss Lady, Kupenda is on line 4"

"Thank you Ronnie."

"Greetings, Kupenda, this is Isis. I know I'm probably the last person you'd be expecting to hear from, however, I wanted to take this opportunity to extend an olive branch of peace. I know we've had our run ins over the last 2-3 years and I totally accept full accountability and responsibility for my actions. With that being said, I must ask, do you have a few moments to spare, so we can talk?"

She paused with reservation whether or not to finish out the conversation, then I heard a small dainty voice say, "All is well. What on earth did I do to deserve a phone call from the notorious Wedding Crasher? Got any more weddings to ruin?"

"Ok, ok, I"ll take that however this call between us is not what you think it is. Do you recall that day at the gas station and I told you to submit a resume, etc.?"

"Yeah, what about it?"

"Well, do you have a resume? The only reason I'm asking is because we just hired a new real estate agent and she needs an assistant, so I thought of you. Might as well get all the blacks in here at one time while no one is looking."

Saying a small joke to try to alleviate the tension on the phone, it actually worked because she started to laugh.

Kupenda responds, "Yes, I recall. And yes, I have a resume."

"Can you get it to Ronnie before the end of the day?"

"I sure can. I can send it over when we hang up. But before we go, can I ask you why you thought of me for the assistant position?"

"The reason I thought of you is because I'm strategizing on building a power real estate team and with your snazzy attitude along with all that comes with it, I thought you'd be perfect. So, do you accept the offer? No worries about compensation. That's going to all be taken care of and before you ask, no I'm not paying pennies. Are there any other questions?"

"Yes, what are the days, times, and the dress code?"

"Days and times will be Monday - Friday, business casual, except for Friday, we have a relaxed day, but no gym shoes. Also, are you busy around 5:00 this afternoon? Maybe we can all meet and get to know each other, since we'll all be working closely together. How does that sound to you?"

"Well, that sounds like a plan. If I think of any more questions, I'll be sure to write them down so that way you can address them at the meet and greet. And where will we meet and greet?"

"You know I'm not sure, let me have Ronnie do some digging and I'll have him call you with the information. Does that work?"

"Indeed, I'll be waiting for the call. Thank you so much, Isis. I appreciate you for this opportunity."

Then, the call was terminated.

Now, I don't know what I just put in this mixture, but whatever it is, it's got to work out for my benefit. But wait, what do I stand to gain by mixing Horisha and Kupenda. I mean after-all, the only thing they have in common is Lance and I need Kupenda to try to squeeze any information out of her future boss to see what her real motive is. Now, the plot twist is telling Avery. I have to let her know about the move I just made, so she doesn't think I'm doing any underhanded business behind her back. So when she does return my call, that'll be the first thing I let her know.

"Ronnie, can you come here please?"

I feel like before I could get the words out of my mouth, he was standing in my doorway. For whatever reason, he always has this pleasant smile on his face. It's almost as if he really enjoys his job. For that very reason, he's gonna train Kupenda and get her right where I need her to be.

"Yes, Boss Lady, what can I do for you?"

"Well have a seat, no need for note taking. I'm about to fill you in, professionally, got it?"

Pulling up a chair, he sat down at the edge of my desk, but he faced the window to check out the view.

"What needs to be done?"

"Well, as you know, Mr. Donahue hired Horisha. She's taking our old office. He said I needed to find her an assistant and you need to train them. So, you pretty much got an idea as to what I just did."

With a look of intensity, he said, "You hired Kupenda? I have to train her?"

I responded, "I did. Is there something wrong with that?"

"No, not at all. I mean you weren't always the nicest when the two of you saw each other. Now, you turned around and offered her a job. I mean what's the common denominator?"

"Well, I think I know, but I'm not so sure just yet. That's why I need to strategically play my hand. It's chess, not checkers."

"Ok. Well, in that case, let's play to win. But one day, you have to tell me who the pieces are, so I get a better understanding as to how you're playing this game."

"Of course, no worries. But for now, I need you to contact Horisha and see if she'll be free around 5 this evening for a meet and greet with the new crew. The new crew being you, Kupenda, her and I. Once you've confirmed that, find a central location that is feasible for everyone to access, and we'll discuss the details later. Oh! Pull the new hire information from HR, the new realtor and new assistant forms."

"I'm already ahead of you in that arena. I did that when you first told me after you came back from the interview. I even contacted security and the key cards are being created for pick up within the next few days."

"Well, damn, look at you. Also, before I forget, this is between you and I. Mr. Donahue is retiring and wants to leave the firm to me. I haven't given him an answer yet. I'm still on the fence because you know I want my own real estate agency."

"Oh my goodness, that's dope. I mean, if he is leaving it to you, then just have a huge party to let everybody know it's yours. Think about it. It's already established and everybody knows who you are here. Regardless, whatever you do or wherever you go, take my black ass with you. But, remember what Granny used to say, 'Universe, show me what I need to see.'"

"Just ask the universe to let you know if it's the right decision for you to make and above all, do what feels right. If you don't need anything else, I'm headed back to my desk to find a spot for the meet and greet."

"Thank you, that'll be all. Oh, there's one more thing before you leave, I appreciate you."

"Well, show your appreciation in my check with a bonus."

While he exited, we laughed as he went to handle the rest of his to-do-list. Of course, I had some things to mull over in my mind.

Where is Kareem when I need him? I swear he'd know what to do. Just as I was getting ready to get irritated, it hit me. Horisha, if that's her homeboy from way back, maybe she has heard from him or knows his whereabouts. Yeah, I don't know. I don't want her knowing too much about my personal business, especially when it comes to Kareem. So, let me 86 that idea and relax. He's always said, if something happened to him, there would be people in place to let me know what's up. Guess I better trust the theory.

As time is passing by, I still haven't heard from Avery. Let me reach out again. This is not like her. I would've heard from her by now. Leaning over to pick up my cell phone, I noticed that she and Kareem both had called me. That was truly a weight lifted off my shoulders. At least, now I know that he's alright and she was probably somewhere checking up on Lance. Now, let me call Kareem back because I know his ass better have a damn good explanation as to where the fuck he dipped off to. It's been almost 3 weeks. That shit is abnormal for any human being to be tucked away so far in the center of the earth that they don't check in. Oh, no worries, he's going to hear it from me when I talk to him.

Before I could calm my nerves and not be so pissed, Ronnie yells out, "Boss, it's a call on line 4. I think it's Kareem."

"Thank you, Ronnie"

Picking up the phone without a relieved smile on my face was hard to do, especially when he knows me so well. I gotta let him know I'm super pissed off.

"Isis speaking. How can I be of service to you?"

"First of all, you can put that fictitious attitude to the side. Hear me out, so you'll understand where I've been."

"Nigga, if you think for one second that you gone try to sweet talk me, so I can let you off the hook, then yo' ass got another thing coming. Where the fuck have you been? It's been almost 3 weeks, if not 4. Why the fuck haven't you picked up a phone, shot a text, or used a courier pigeon? Hell, at this point, you could've put a fucking message in a bottle. Reaching out ain't that hard. This is some extreme fuckery, and you know it. So, you better have a damn good reason as to why I haven't heard from you. Too much has been going on. COVID is running wild and you have been missing in action. I don't even know where to begin to start."

As I was finally getting a moment to take a deep breath, before I began to start going in again, he interrupted me.

He said, as calmly as only he could, "I was in Vegas doing a show. The producer, Sinclair Roman, known for producing Krave and Big Thick. He set up a meeting with us and we got signed to a deal with GMM."

I guess I could no longer be mad, because he was calling with good news and I should be happy for him. I guess I can share my good news with him, as well. But, I still don't want him to think he's off the hook just yet.

"Since we're sharing good news, after the run-in that Ronnie had with De'Angelo, Mr. Donahue moved us to the penthouse suite, and to top it off he offered to leave the company to me when he retires. That would mean Keys Real Estate would be changed to Carrington and Associates. Furthermore, speaking of associates, Mr. Donahue hired Horisha. Ronnie is getting her an assistant that will be trained and well versed in the real estate protocols. She starts Monday. We're going out later today, so she can meet her new assistant."

"Well damn, little one, you said a whole mouth full. I'm glad yo' shit is coming up just like you want it too. Is everything else alright? What do I need to be caught up on?"

"Nothing at the moment. That was it other than panicking because I hadn't heard from you. I was almost getting ready to roll past Mya house to see if anything looks suspicious."

"Naw, I haven't talked to her, since we got into it about the bullshit she pulled with that money. Yeah, it's safe to say it's over with her. I got shit to prove to my future wife."

"Nigga, I done told you to stop playing with me. Yo' ass is too damn calculated just to be running off some random ass statements like that."

"Since you know me so well, then why the hell are you still on that bullshit? Just be ready when I get my ass on one knee for you. Besides I told you once I secured the bag, it was me and you. Bag secured. Now, it's time for me to secure you."

"I hear you talking, but there's other things we need to discuss, and if I'm correct, you're still at the airport. So, hit me when you touch down. I should be home by 9. Are you coming through?"

"Yep, as soon as I check on my two OGs, but I'll call you when I'm headed your way. Oh yeah, is surveillance still on the street?"

"Yeah and when will you tell them to leave?"

"The minute I touch down, I can deliver the message in person. I think that situation should be resolved by now. Yeah. Don't even think to ask no questions. Love you little one. See you in a minute."

KeanaMonique

Well, I'll be damned. I can't believe that he outsmarted me and my attitude. I hate that he knows me as well as he does. Since he's taken care of and I know what was up with him, I need to call Avery back. As soon as I start to pick up the phone, Ronnie enters the office and lets me know he has made reservations at the Oyster Bowl.

"Um, excuse me, but isn't that a bit pricey? I'm not paying for everyone's food, if we go there. Besides we just want to do something quick, so the two of them can get slightly acquainted. How about you call the Grey Bistro instead?"

"Oh, I forgot about them. I'll call them after I cancel the reservation at the Oyster Bowl."

"Don't forget to make sure the two are available. There is no sense in meeting if the two that are supposed to meet aren't available."

He gave me the thumbs up, and he went on his way.

Now, if I can get to my plans, I need to call Avery and see what she knows, if anything. I also need to let her know that I've hired Horisha and Kupenda. I had to laugh to myself, because this shit is going to be funny. But, it all depends on her reaction. Her phone is ringing, and for whatever reason I'm getting nervous, and my palms are starting to sweat.

"Hey, girl! It's Isis. What's good with you?"

"Oh my goodness, what's not going on? I just got a call from the school saying that prom and graduation are canceled because someone contracted COVID. It also said the quarantine curfew time exceeds the prom and graduation. Needless to say, the children are bummed out. So, I'm trying to figure out what they can do in spite of the prom and graduation."

"Well, if you need anything in that arena just let me know."

Thinking to myself how surprised I am that Ryan hasn't sent me a text message stating the obvious, or maybe he's waiting to see me in person. Hell, who knows? All I know is the fact that Avery had to spill the beans and this is the second time I heard from her instead of my son is a problem. But, that's alright.

I'll fix this issue when I make it back to the house.

"So, tell me some good news Isis."

"Well, I don't know how good the news is, but I need to bring you up to speed on the recent current events."

"Do tell. I'm listening."

"Today, Horirsha had her interview and Mr. Donahue hired her. He also told me to have Ronnie find her an assistant."

Avery interrupts, "Ok…so, I'm unsure why you're telling me, so make it make sense."

"I'll just say, Ronnie is gonna train Kupenda as her assistant."

There was a short brief silence on the phone before and I wasn't sure if she lost signal or if she hung up or what.

"Avery are you there? Hello, Avery?"

"Well, I'll be damned. If that ain't some good shit right there, you just put both of Lance's whores in the same office. Now tell me, what's the gag?"

"Well, you know Kupenda is tight with Ronnie. She tells him everything, so if Ronnie can persuade Kupenda to get all chummy with her boss, then Kupenda can let us know the underlying scheme with Horisha. Once we know how she is planning to navigate through this media frenzy bullshit, we can be two steps ahead of her. Do you get it now?"

"Hell yeah", Avery said in excitement, "Girl, that was pure genius."

"Ronnie and I are planning a meet up this evening, so the two of them can get acquainted and hopefully form a connection because they will be working together."

"When you finalize it, let me know. I want to be there."

"No! You cannot come. Horisha would recognize you from The Blue Room incident and that'll spoil it. But, I'll definitely keep you posted and send a few texts from time to time. Sounds good?"

"Indeed. Keep me posted and I'll just talk to you later. I gotta get back to figuring out what they are going to do with the prom situation. Enjoy the meal."

That went over extremely well with Avery and Kareem too. I am unsure on how to feel about both of them being so easy going, or maybe I'm missing something. But, nevertheless, I'm relieved that Kareem is ok. Well, Avery is....Avery. Laughing to myself, while thinking what I just pulled off was pure genius, in walks Ronnie.

"Boss Lady, I've touched bases with Kupenda and Horisha. They both agreed to meet us at the Grey Bistro around 5. The previous reservation has been canceled and a new one is set. Is there anything else I can do to assist you before we leave for this meet and greet?"

"I can't think of anything at the moment, but thank you. Oh, there is one thing. Check your email and see if Kupenda sent over her resume. Print it out, so I can attach it to her file for HR. Also, grab Horisha's file when you're finished and set both of them on my desk."

Finalizing all the loose ends before we leave, I take a moment and think about the upcoming events that could possibly take place. I know mixing the two of these women may mean potential disaster, but something has to give. I can't go to Kareem and ask about Horisha. She's not that comfortable yet to go telling *all* her business to me. But, I don't know. She did just drop a bomb on me so unexpectedly. That information I still have yet to process. I haven't even begun to apply it to the situation. I know Lance has made a fucking mess of this whole clusterfuck of a situation, and as usual, women to the rescue.

But, I can't believe that he has a son that's almost 20 years old. Man, shit, when Avery finds out that Aniya ain't the only child of his, it's going to be hell to pay. Damn, it's going to be hell to pay either way because if she finds out that I knew it's going to be over. I have no idea what she may do. Then again, we are talking about Avery Whitaker and hell, she may already know. Either way it goes, I'm almost, definitely, fucked with no Vaseline.

Chapter 17

The Grey Bistro

Feeling somewhat relaxed about the events of the day, I still can't seem to figure out why Mr. Donahue is retiring and why he wants to turn the office over to me. However, I can see it crystal clear now, that sign reads "Carrington & Associates". That'll look exceptionally well on the marquee outside the building. Hell, I may be able to do it real big and have a few of those billboards that Avery had a few months back. Either way it goes, whatever I do, I gotta go all out. I gotta do it big.

"Boss Lady, where did you journey off to? We've been sitting in the car for a few moments and you just checked out on me. Is everything alright with you?"

Snapping back into reality, "Of course I'm ok, just listening to the ancestral messages for the meet and greet. I just hope all goes well and no one ends up fighting."

"Boss Lady, don't you think we're a bit too old to be fighting. Now, a bitch can always catch these hands, but I try to always talk myself out of fighting unless..."

Before he could finish, I took the opportunity to gut punch him

"I just bet you can throw those hands, but where were those hands when DeAngelo was jumping on you? All I heard was a high-pitched scream and you saying, 'Boss Lady, come get this nigga off me.'"

With a slight look of embarrassment, Ronnie replied, "Too Soon."

Laughing uncontrollably, I know it made him feel uncomfortable, so being quick on my feet, I had to smooth things over before this meet and greet started off with the wrong energy.

"Ronnie, I am sorry. I know how sensitive that subject matter is for you. It was extremely premature for me to take it there. Will you accept my apology?"

With an unrecognizable look, he turned to me and said, "Oh no apologies necessary, but know when the time comes I'm coming for you. Be prepared."

He smirked and said, "Now, let's get to this meeting before they do, so we have control of the room."

In some weird way, I knew he was hurt deep down. He always has my back and knows what to say to keep me on task. But for whatever reason, I need to be on my shit because he knows exactly when to push the right buttons. As we were driving from the office, I couldn't help but put on some ratchet music, so I could be in a different mindset. The best way, to do such, is to relax myself. I hope this makes Ronnie also become relaxed after that joke I pulled. Then, we can go into this and do what needs to be done. I hate to feel like I'm scheming, but it kind of is. I really gotta know what Horisha's motive is. I mean does she know how all of us are connected? Did Kareem tell her anything other than what he said he told her? How does she plan to tell Lance? Should I tell Avery about the meeting in detail? It's too many questions going on in my head. I need to have a drink.

"Ronnie, can you go through my playlist and play me anything 2pac?"

He turned, looked at me, and said, "Ok, Isis, 2pac? He wasn't even alive when I was born. Can we listen to something from my lifetime?"

"Color me baffled, but yo' momma was pregnant when he died, and she knows about him. So, you alright by default. Now, just play me something, so I can get my mind right."

"Look at the ancient ratchetness trying to come out," jokes Ronnie.

"Just so you know, it's not ancient. It's classic. Now, come on. We got to go in here and prepare our next winning team for Carrington & Associates. You know the drill right?"

Ronnie responds, "Of course, I do. Let me do me and you handle Horisha. That's the plan. We got this. Speaking of us having the situation, looks like we are a few minutes late. There's Kupenda, and she's on time. Look at her all dressed up, looking like she is ready to go to work. She Ready!"

We laugh. I say, "Ok. Tiffany Haddish."

As I turn to the left, I see Horisha has made it to the restaurant. I guess she arrived a few minutes after we did. Had we not been here when we arrived, we would have missed the parking lot runway show. Look at the two of them, Horisha and Kupenda stepping and getting ready to walk into the corporate world of real estate. I can't wait to build this team

"Ronnie, let's get this show on the road and let's see what's cooking."

Exiting the vehicle, I'm stepping out just as sexy as the other girls, maybe sexier, if I do say so myself. Of course, there's my ace-in-the-hole, Ronnie. To me, I mean, this looks like the money team getting ready to get to work. As we all walked from our perspective parking spots, we kind of all had this weird smile like each one of us had our own hidden agendas. Actually, we all do. That's why we're here, so I can stay ahead of the plot.

As Ronnie grabbed the door for the ladies, the hostess greeted us with a smile and said, "Welcome to the Grey Bistro. Do you have reservations?"

"Yes. Carrington for 4 at 5."

"I'm assuming that your party is all here. Follow me and I'll get you seated."

As we're walking to our table, I can hear Kupenda saying to Ronnie, "I hope I'm not overdressed. I just want to make sure I impress her, so she doesn't have to second guess giving me the job."

As Ronnie looked her up and down, he said out loud for all to hear, "Bitch, you real sexy for a muthafucka that just got hired today."

Kupenda playfully hits him and they start laughing. I turn around, look, and give her a smile just to let her know she's good.

"Your server will be with you shortly," said the hostess as she walked away.

"Let me get the introductions out the way, so we can get down to business. Horisha, meet Kupenda.

She is your new office assistant. Kupenda, meet Horisha. She is your new boss."

Pleasantries were exchanged and everything was going well. As the waiter came by, I took the lead and ordered martinis for everyone. I just want to ease any possible nervousness.

"I don't want to keep you all for too long. I just wanted to say a few things and let everyone know what's going on. Horisha, you already know you've been hired as a new agent to the company. Kupenda, you have just learned you'll be her assistant. Ronnie will train you to be the best assistant possible."

Before I could finish, Ronnie interrupts me by saying, "Boss Lady, I'm the best. I'm sorry. It don't get no better than me. But, I'll show her what she needs to know."

And typical Ronnie, on time with the interruption, because it made everyone laugh.

"I just want you all to know, in the near future there will be some changes in the structural set up of Keys Real Estate Agency, but as long as we're on the same page we'll be good. Just understand that we are a team and if we have any issues we come to each other. As long as we have that understanding, then everything will go smoothly. Now, that I've got that out the way. Let's just enjoy the evening and we'll all be in the same building within the next 72 hours."

I'll call it perfect timing because our waiter brought our drinks right after I finished my statement. Let's lift our glasses and toast to the winning team, Carrington & Associates. As we toasted to the new team, in walks Lance Whitaker.

With a slight look of disgust, I just wonder which one of now, which one of these heffas contacted him because this is so fucking random. But, maybe it's a good thing, so I can see the body language and facial expressions of all three of them- Kupenda, Horisha, and of course, Lance. As I'm checking out the scenery, he appears to be alone, which is odd because his thot boxes are with me and Avery is nowhere in the vicinity. Ah, maybe she sent him on some strange shit. That doesn't make sense because she needs to know the information I get from the meeting. Why is he here?

All I can think is please don't come over here, please don't come over here. Those are the only words that seem to be on repeat in my mind. As I already knew, he walked over to the table and fortunately for me. Ronnie was the only other person who saw him because the way the tables were set up, the other's had their backs to the door.

Before he could startle the girls, Ronnie stood up and said, "Mr. Whitaker, what a surprise, are you joining us or will you be dining alone?"

That alerted both of them. They both turned around and I'll just say, it went in a totally different direction than I had played out in my mind.

"Hello everyone, I just came to have a few drinks myself, alone of course, but I saw Isis. I mean, Ms. Carrington, so I decided to come and speak."

I think this may be the first time Horisha has seen Lance, since she's been home and she conducted herself just as a woman. She and Kupenda both held it together well.

Horisha said, "Hello, Mr. Whitaker, how are you?"

Kupenda followed suit, as she turned around, she spoke as well. They both turned back around and proceeded to act unbothered by his presence. It's almost as if it was planned because it was so on que it couldn't have been timed any better than that. As he acknowledged both of them, in the same breath he bidded us a good evening and walked away. Now, if I didn't know any better I'd have to say he wasn't surprised, but him bumping into the chairs behind him was a dead giveaway, that clearly that nigga was caught off guard.

When he was seated, Ronnie said, “Well, what in the entire fuck was that? I mean, damn, he almost fell trying to get away from this table.”

We laughed quietly, so we wouldn’t alert him to turn around and look.

Then out of nowhere Horisha says, “He got it coming. He just doesn’t know it yet.

On que again, Kupenda says, “You got that right, Boss.”

They looked at one another with a sideway smile and together they sipped.

As we concluded our meet and greet, we all went our separate ways. As I’m in the car going with the flow of traffic, I feel more confident that we are going to be a great support system to one another and make money in the real estate game. I do believe that we, despite our previous paths that allowed us to get here, are definitely going to be great together.

Interrupting my thoughts as usual, Ronnie states, “Boss Lady, I swear you stay drifting on a memory, where did you go this time?”

Laughing slightly, it's oddly cute that he knows me as well as he does.

"I'm good just thinking about the decision to bring those two on board and the backlash that may come behind it."

"What backlash are you talking about?"

" I mean if anybody finds out that I'm behind all this, then everything I've worked so hard for is going to go to hell in a handbasket."

"Boss Lady, I don't know all the secrets you hold, but if it helps you sleep at night, then I'm here and we gone go through and get through all of this together. So, if you wanna talk about it or if you don't, I'm here. Standing right beside you."

"Wow, Ronnie, I really appreciate that. As I pull up to Ronnie's residence, I smile at him and tell "Go ahead, get inside, and get some rest. We have a full day ahead of us tomorrow."

"You're right, Boss Lady. You do the same. I'll see you in the office in the morning."

Chapter 18

Strickland

Driving towards home, I just know I need to keep my ducks in a row, and I'm sure everything will work in my favor. With Mr. Donahue retiring, Horisha having a manchild by Lance, Kupenda is on my team, Avery not knowing about the love child of Lance and Horisha, then you've got the fact that Kareem is being weird to me, talking marriage and shit, oh and not to mention, Ryan is not really communicating with me about the graduation or prom shit. I'm fucking over it. But, I know I need to keep my head above water and my feet planted firmly on the ground to be able to pull off this major move.

Lo and behold as I pull up to the house, as usual, I notice cars. Without second guessing, I see Aniya's car and there's another car that is unfamiliar. So now I'm wondering, who does he have in my damn house? I swear I don't know what has gotten into Ryan, but this ain't like him.

Entering the house, I see Dino running around the house with the game headphones on and talking to whoever it is in cyber land and as I approach the kitchen, I see Strickland. What the entire fuck is really going on and how does he know Ryan?

"Hey, Ma dukes! What's good? We already ate and I wanted you to meet a new friend of mine. His name is Strickland."

As we are being reintroduced to one another, I played it cool and kept my game face on. I wanted to be real observant about what is about to take place.

Strickland starts to speak, "Hi, Miss Carrington. You have a lovely home."

"Thank you so much, so how do you know Ryan and Aniya?"

"Well, I met Ryan a few weeks back on the basketball court over at the park and we hit it off. Today, he asked if I wanted to hang with him and Aniya over here. So, I told him, let me check in with my mom and I'll get with him. My moms said yeah and here I am. Small world, huh?"

"Indeed," I replied, "I hope you all are enjoying yourself. Ryan let me talk to you in the other room real quick."

As we got to my bedroom, I instantly went in.

"Can you tell me a few things? Why did I have to find out about the prom situation from Avery and why didn't you tell me? Secondly, you can't be bringing strays to our home. You don't know this young man, and I don't want you to get all caught up in something you have no knowledge of. Now, I'm listening. What's good? Why haven't you been talking to me?"

"Ma, you been real busy with work. Every time you come home, I just be excited to see you and that shit, I mean stuff, just slipped my mind. I'm sorry. But, now you know the prom and graduation is canceled, due to COVID. We're unsure of what we're going to do about it. That's nothing we can handle. Right now, it's out of our hands. We just gotta wait and see what the school says about it."

At this point, I kinda shrug and roll my eyes. He has a point. But, that doesn't mean I'm still not upset about his not communicating with me. So, I continue to listen.

Ryan goes on, "And as far as bringing strays home, Strickland is real cool. You know his granny, Mrs. Harper, the lady that you met at the place y'all be getting y'all eyebrows done at."

Still angry, I chime in, "I know, damn well, you ain't telling me that his grandmother is the sassy woman with the Land Rover and the salt and pepper hair?"

"Yeah, that's her. I saw her drop him off at the basketball court and I asked him who she was. He said that was his granny and she raised him because his mom was in prison."

Touching his shoulder, I said to him, "Baby, be careful. This world is too small and you just never know who you run into. Some people have different agendas and you just never know what's what. Although he may be cool, you make sure you keep Aniya safe at all times when y'all are together. Just look out for her, please."

"Alright. Mom, but you're scaring me. Is everything alright?"

"Yes, baby. Just promise to protect her at all costs. You got me? In your terms, ya dig?"

As we both laughed out loud, we hugged and went on back into the kitchen to see what was going on.

"Hey! What yall got going on? You three, pointing at Dino, Aniya and Ryan, yall got school tomorrow and although y'all may be seniors, Dino ain't. You, my buddy, have school tomorrow. Finish this up and don't be up too long. Strickland, it was nice meeting you. Since you and Ryan are homies, I guess I'll be seeing more of you."

I pause and look around the room to check everything out.

I turn and say, "I'm headed to do some work in the den, so if I'm needed you know where I am."

Walking away, Ryan says, "Hey! Aren't you forgetting something?"

With a twisted look on my face I ask, "What?"

Before I could say anything else, the three of three of them–Ryan, Dino and Aniya–came running up to hug me and give me kisses.

Dino then says, "Mommy, don't forget your mommy juice."

As we all started laughing, Ryan said, "I'll grab the bottle. Aniya, grab her glass."

I swear my children and bonus daughter really know how to lay it on thick.

Sitting in the den, with my computer and cell phone, I couldn't help but wonder if Strickland knows what's up or is he just caught up in living his life? Does he truly have no idea that Aniya is his baby sister? Looking at them, they have a very similar resemblance to each other. Both have chocolate skin, thick eyebrows, and deep wavy hair. Lance knows he has some strong genes and I swear I don't want Ryan to get caught up in nothing he truly knows nothing about. I would blow the world up if my son becomes a casualty of somebody else's war. Now that I know another piece of the puzzle just fell in my lap, I swear this rabbit hole just gets deeper and deeper. What the fuck?

I have to call Kareem. I swear he better make sense of this. First, let me get my toilet-sex-having ass in the shower. Laughing out loud, that damn Ronnie. I swear he be on top of his shit. To think, my colleagues told me hiring a homosexual would not be a good look for the company. Guess we showed them.

Before I jump in the shower, I send Kareem a text message letting him know it was urgent that I speak with him. After that I pulled out some comfy pajamas and headed into the shower. As the water raced down my skin, I lathered up my loofa to wash off the secrets of today, I couldn't help but to think about how I was actually fucking in the public bathroom in the mall. Although it was an extreme turn on and so spontaneous, it made me rethink my decision to fuck with Jaylen.

Yeah, he's younger than me and he is De'Angelo's nephew. But, that little nigga got dick for days. Soaping up and cleansing myself, I heard a knock on the bathroom door. Rinsing off and turning the water off, I hurried up and grabbed my bath robe to go unlock the door and to my surprise it was Kareem.

"How did you get in?"

"Through the front door," He says with a big ass smile on his face.

"Clearly, I'm aware of that. I guess I mean, how did you get here so fast? I just texted you and said it was urgent. I wasn't expecting you to show up. I thought you might have been at the studio or doing whatever it is that you do when you're not here with me."

"Little one, I was actually leaving the studio headed here when you sent the text, so I just showed up. I walked up as the lil homie and Aniya was leaving out the door. Ryan let me in. So, what was so urgent? What's wrong? You good?"

"Well not really, I got some questions and you got the answers."

"Are you sure I do?"

"Hell yeah, I'm sure. For starters, did you know Horisha had a 20-year-old son?, who happened to be the lil homie you saw leaving the house?"

With a look of total confusion, he told me no.

"Kareem, don't lie to me."

Looking at me with a very serious look on his face, he replied, " I ain't never lied to you before and I don't appreciate that you just accused me of lying to you at this moment."

"Well, from what I know, Horisha was pregnant and had the baby while she was incarerated . Her mother raised him. Final shocker, her son is Lance Whitaker's son."

"Who is Lance Whitaker?"

"The hoe ass dude she took the charge for."

"Well, she never told me the nigga name, so I don't know who he is. Why is her son coming out of the crib?"

"Before I get to that I'll say this. Lance is married to Avery and they have a daughter named Aniya, who happens to be Ryan's girlfriend. Ryan met him while playing basketball and they hit it off. Now, I won't be the one to tell Aniya that Ryan's new homie is her half brother, but I did tell Ryan to protect Aniya at all cost because I don't know what Strickland's motive is."

"Who is Strickland?"

"Remember Lil homie? Come on. Keep up. Now, to top it all off, Avery, Aniya's mom, and I are honing in on a friendship. I don't know how to tell her what I just found out by putting pieces together."

"Damn, that's a lot, for starters, you did right by telling Ryan to look out for his shorty, and as far as Avery is concerned, you don't know shit about Horisha, other than what is going on in the news. That way you'll keep your hands clean and let whoever finds out whatever on their own terms."

"Is it that simple and easy?"

"Yeah, if you stick to the program. Unless you tell or told someone else, who's gonna say you lying about what you know."

"I guess you might be right."

"I ain't steered you wrong yet, just trust me. I'll see what else I can find out. But for right now, I'm tired and it appears that you are getting ready for bed, so let's cuddle and go to sleep."

Who would have thought that cuddling would be so satisfying, laying here on his tattooed chest. The more I listened to his heartbeat the more our rhythm became in sync with each other. The more I tried to get comfortable the more all the thoughts kept arising in my mind. They say that you truly do have that one person in the world that's made just for you. They understand you. They finish your sentences. They love you unconditionally. Most importantly, the two of you are friends.

It makes me wonder what would change, if he actually asked me to marry him. If I say yes, would it change the dynamics of our relationship? Would we still be who we are in marriage as we are right now? I guess that's a lot to think about, but only time will tell.

Before I drifted off to sleep, I whispered those words "I love you Kareem," and with perfect timing he replied " I love you too, little one."

He grabbed me tighter, kissed me on my neck and we went to sleep.

Chapter 19

Avery

Still cuddled up, I should say tangled up. As I look at our bodies, I swear I can't tell my skin from his. This is my person and I'm his person, flaws and all.

Now, it's time to be playful. I wiggled away from his embrace. I went to look for my cell phone and make sure my children are getting ready for school.

"Good morning, OG," Ryan says as he hands Dino his breakfast sandwich.

"Hey! How are my two favorite people in the world?"

Dino replied, "Don't you mean three? You can't forget Kareem," laughing hysterically.

"Well, Kareem is not in the kitchen, so he doesn't count."

"Mommy, guess what? Today, we are going to the mall with Kareem and I'm going to pick out," before he could finish his sentence, Ryan interrupted him and said "His favorite pair of shoes, as long as he passes his spelling test. Ain't that right?"

Dino looked confused as he took a bite of his sandwich and said, "Yep. I gotta pass my spelling test."

"Well in that case, did you study?"

"Yes, Aniya and Ryan helped me work really hard to get a good grade today."

"I'll be expecting a big A on the test paper, so we can put it right on the refrigerator when you get home this afternoon."

As I turned and looked at Ryan, I asked him, "Did I make myself clear in the conversation we had last night?"

"Indeed," said Ryan as he confirmed with a head nod.

I gave them both a kiss as they left for school.

After I saw them out, I grabbed my cell phone and noticed that I had a few calls from Avery and Ronnie. I also had a call from an unfamiliar number. I'll handle that when I get in the car.

As I opened up my bedroom door, I was immediately hit with a pillow.

"Well damn, I thought you were sleep?"

"I was until I turned over to grab you and you weren't there."

"I just saw the boys out before they went to school. Dino mentioned that you were going to get him some shoes, if he passes his spelling test?"

With a slightly aggravated look he said, "Yeah, that was part of the deal."

"And what was the other part?"

"None of yo' damn business, Nosy."

"Well whatever, what's on your agenda for the day?"

"Uh, The mall, obviously."

"Ugh, you make me sick."

"Aye, why didn't you ride the rollercoaster last night?"

"If it had been operational, then I probably would have, If I didn't know any better, then I'd swear by you being gone all that time that you had already let somebody ride the rollercoaster."

"Yeah, I could've said the same thing to you too. You probably let somebody hit it while I was gone."

"Nigga whatever."

Thinking to myself, that was the perfect opportunity to tell him the truth, but shit that nigga know me too well. So whatever, if he ain't coming to me with no proof that I did what I did, then it didn't happen. I know he feels the same way.

"Just make sure you get on it tonight when I get home."

"Home?" I said with a sarcastic tone.

"Yeah, you heard what I said. Make sure you come straight here after work."

"Um, when did you start making demands like that?"

"I've always done it. You've always listened, so don't start questioning me now."

I try to look unphased and say, "I do have some errands to run after work, so I'll be here when I get finished."

"Like I said, just get here and don't be all night. Where's your piece at?"

"In the night stand, why what's up?"

"You know the weather is breaking and niggas starting to act a fool. I don't wanna have to start this new chapter off all wrong."

I ask, "What new chapter? I swear since you've been back from Vegas you've been talking differently and shit. What's up with you?"

"Just know I'm calculated. Case closed. Gone get ready for work. I'm about to roll and I'll be back later."

He kissed me on my forehead, smacked me on my ass, and left.

Now, I'm really wondering what in the entire fuck is going on? I know I gotta keep my head in the game. I'm about to have my own real estate company. I'm building a power team. My oldest son is finishing high school and heading on to his next life journey, and my baby boy is growing up right before my eyes. What else could possibly be going on out here in the universe? Clearly, I have enough shit going on. Let me shower and get ready for work.

Stepping out in my sexy navy-blue Christian Dior two-piece business suit, I swear I feel like I'm about to conquer the world. The sun is shining, birds are chirping and I swear I just love the sound of woodpeckers. Although those pesky things can rarely be seen, the sound they make just does something to my spirit.

Standing barefoot on the ground, showing gratitude to the universe, my session is ruined by the ringing of my cell phone. Trying not to answer it with an irritated voice, I quickly snap out of it and answer it with a smile, so my smile can be heard through the phone. Gotta keep those positive vibes flowing.

"Good morning, Isis Carrington speaking."

"Girl, this is Avery, I need some information from you."

As I'm hesitating to ask what it is, she goes from hyped up to almost in tears.

"Ok, I'm unsure how to respond, at first you seemed excited. Now, I hear the cracking of your voice as if to say you might be hurting. Are you good?"

Putting my shoes on and hurrying into the truck, she begins to speak.

"Everything is happening so fast. I know I got a lot of irons in the fire, but this one is too hot to contain. Last night, we were all at home. It was myself, Lance, and Aniya. We were just shooting the shit and the news came on and that mess with Lance came up. Although Aniya knows her daddy ain't shit, she really only knows from her lifetime perspective, so when the news came on I tried to change the channel. Before I could change it, she saw a photo of Lance from 20 years ago. The same picture that's been floating around ever since that Horisha chick came home. I looked at him. He tried to play it off. He looked as if he didn't care that she was about to hear something detrimental. At least, he sat there willing to explain himself, in case she had any questions. But, what came out of her mouth was something I had no knowledge of. He didn't confirm or deny the allegations. I don't know what to do, say, or think."

At this time, if my intuition serves me correctly, then the photo from 20 years ago of Lance that was seen on the news, has to heavily resemble Strickland. I'm thinking Aniya had to put it together. I'm really hoping that's not what she's about to tell me.

"Well, I'm kind of afraid to ask what was it that came out of her mouth, but do tell."

"The way she started off was as if she was talking about something totally unrelated, then she grabbed her cell phone and laptop. She googled the image of her dad, and pulled up her cell phone and showed us a picture of her, Ryan and a young man named, Strickland. She said Ryan met Strickland on the basketball court and the two of them became fast friends. Now, they have been hanging together."

Before she could finish, I interrupted her by saying, "Yeah, I just met him last night when I came home and saw him there. I don't know anything about him other than Ryan told me his grandmother's name is Mrs. Harper. I know she drives a Land Rover and she gets her eyebrows done at the same place as me. But, what is the connection?"

I have to play along like I have no idea what is about to come out of Avery's mouth. She is Avery. If she senses that I know, then Kareem's suggested plan will be right out the damn window. The goal is to not get on her bad side.

I continue, "It's almost as if he just popped up out of nowhere. I mean Ryan has been playing ball at that park for years and all the neighborhood fellas know him. But, this boy just appeared from out of nowhere. It's hardly unlikely. I'm sorry I interrupted you. Let's put these pieces together."

As she laughed she said, "If I didn't know any better, I would swear you were holding out on some information about my no-good husband."

In my reply, I asked, "What do you mean about your husband? I'm confused. What does this have to do with Lance?"

"Ok, back to the story, so Aniya pulled up the photo of Lance and showed us a picture of all three of them. I'll be God damned if this little nigga didn't look just like Lance. Eyebrows, skin complexion, and the facial structure looks exactly like Lance. Shit, him and Aniya favor as well. So, she asked him if he had something he wanted to share with us? He looked at both pictures and said, nope. In her eyes, he can do no wrong. She took it as if he would never lie to her, and she kept it moving. But me being her mother, she shot me both images with a wink emoji. If that ain't my father's granddaughter, I don't know who she is. It's almost like he has been reincarnated in her, 'cause the shit she's been doing lately is almost as if my father is still walking the streets."

As I took a deep breath, all I could say was, "What the fuck? So what do you want to do with that information? It's not like it's a secret now. He knows y'all know about this mystery man that just appeared out of nowhere. What do we do now? Well before I go inserting myself in your family business, is there anything you want me to do?"

"Actually, there is. You did mention that Horisha got the job right?"

"Yeah."

"Just keep a close eye on her and see if you hear her talk about a son, or if you see him at the office."

Trying to sound helpful, I ask, "Should I let Ronnie know to tell Kupenda to keep an eye out too or just myself?"

"Shit, you did say she was that girl's new assistant. Hell, I don't want to raise any eyebrows. For now, just keep it to yourself and see what you come up with."

"Your secret is safe with me, I'm actually headed there now a little bit early, so I can go over some stuff with her. But, I'll definitely keep you posted. I'll shoot you a text."

"No! Don't text this, if you get any information call me. I don't want to have receipts just yet. Furthermore, I wanna keep you clean."

"I respect that. I appreciate it. I'll call you when or if I get some information worth sharing. Avery, as hard as it may be, try to keep your cool. You're not alone in this. I got you."

She took a deep breath and replied, "Thank you."

If that nigga, Kareem, wasn't right, I swear, without him knowing the intimate details about whatever situation he is always able to say the right stuff at the right time. Come to think of it, that comment he made about me giving up the cookie to somebody, does he know or is he just talking? That just may be my guilt. If it is, then I'm just going to have to suck it up and keep it moving. Let me put my music on and get my vibe right. That way I will be able to put my best foot forward as I walk up in my new office today. Gotta give Mr. Donahue the confidence that he made the right decision to pass the firm to me.

Chapter 20

The Office

Pulling up to the office, I ran into Ronnie in the parking structure.

"Hey Boss Lady, I called you last night to see if you were watching the news. They showed the story again with Horisha and Lance."

"Yeah, I saw your call. I was wrapped up with the family, and I missed the call as well as the news. Anything good or new from what we already knew?"

"Naw, not really just recapping the story. Have you heard from Horisha?"

"No, she doesn't have my personal number, but she'll be here today to set her office up. When she gets here, we'll just check her vibe to see how she is feeling, but make sure you tell Kupenda to keep an eye out for any new developments."

"Will do. We got some showings today, so let's get in here and make sure we show Mr. Donahue that he made the right choice."

"Get out of my head, I just said the same thing to myself before I got here."

Walking into the office, I ran right into Mr. Donahue, and his face was pale for a Caucasian man.

"Good morning, Mr. Donahue. You look uneasy. Is everything alright?"

"Yes. Everything is fine. There's some paperwork you need to go over and sign, so you can take over. Although, I anticipated a little more time to be here with you. This cancer has come back and there's nothing they can do. So, I'm leaving today."

Surprised and shocked, I replied "Cancer? Wait. What? Which cancer? How long have you had it? What do you mean you're leaving today?"

I had so many questions. My mind was racing.

"I was diagnosed with prostate cancer a few years back, and it went into remission for a time. However, the last four months it has come back with a vengeance. This has been the urgency in leaving the firm to you. I do apologize for that, Isis. I am, now, going home to decide if I'm going to continue treatment or not. There are some things I need to talk over with my family, but everything you need as far as the firm is concerned is all in black and white. Even the papers to change the name from Keys Real Estate to Carrington & Associates. I know you'll be the best fit for the job. Of course, I know I ruffled some feathers with my decision. I recognize that you are the youngest in the firm and a Black woman. Regardless, you have been an asset to this agency. Your skills speak for themselves. Business is business. With your fiery attitude and determination, you will do great, Isis."

Speechless, I replied, "Thank you so much for believing in me and my ability to take on this promotion. I promise I'll do everything I need to do to continue to make this agency the best. I swear I am determined to show you that you made the right decision."

"You've already done that, just continue to do your best work, which is easy for you. You'll be fine."

We parted ways and I was overjoyed with the news. I know today is going to be a fantastic day.

Mr. Donahue sharing he has cancer was shocking. Now, it made more sense why he was moving so quickly. But, I had to chuckle to myself. I thought to myself, even Mr. D knows that I am Isis Muthafuckin' Carrington.

"Ronnie, change of plans. Call down to Horisha's office and have them come up here. I need to call an impromptu meeting to share all the news I just received."

"Certainly, is everything alright?"

"Yes and no, but I'll explain all that at one time when everyone is present. Are there any phone calls I need to return?"

"Well just one, but they didn't leave a message."

"Who calls someone's place of business and doesn't leave a message?"

Before I could get to my office, I remembered the unfamiliar number that came across my phone last night and wondered if the two of them are connected. I really don't need any extra stress. I've already got enough stuff going on and half of it ain't even my business.

Bouncing in my office with that Ronnie-pep always does my spirit good. No matter what goes on, he's always smiling, and I appreciate him for that.

"You got the message for me?"

"I do. I double checked with the answering service to see if it was a male or female to see if they recalled, but they didn't. Is there anything else that you need from me?"

"No, not at the moment, but I'll share the information once everyone is here"

"Alright. Well, I'll be at my desk and when the girls come up we'll all be right in."

Passing me the message before he left, I felt a sudden urge to cross check the unfamiliar number that called my phone last night to the message at the office. Now, if this shit ain't weird. It is the same number, so now I'm skeptical. Whoever this is has my personal number, and they called the office. It's apparent that they want me directly. I have to get to the bottom of this. Taking several deep breaths, I picked up the phone and called the number.

"Hello, Isis Carrington speaking. I'm returning a phone call from Keys Real Estate. Who do I have the pleasure of speaking with?"

The woman's voice on the other end sounded extremely familiar.

"Isis, this is Horisha. I got your cell phone number off the card in the packet I received from HR. I was calling you to speak with you about the events that have been taking place in the news and on social media."

"Are you ok?"

"Yeah. I just needed to get some things off my chest. I apologize for calling you at that hour last night. But with me just getting home, I really didn't have anyone to talk to. Also with you giving me this opportunity to work with you and with the joke you made about Lance being Strickland's father, I figured

I could trust you. As far as I can see you are open minded and observant."

"Horisha, you are, technically, my trainee and I try my best not to cross the lines. Do you want to speak in person when you come up here for the meeting?"

Responding hesitantly, Horisha says, "I prefer not to because that's a work capacity, but since we're on the phone I just wanted you to know I may not be the fit for the company with all this heat on my back about my past. I don't want anything to ruin your chances to take over the company."

"While I do appreciate what you've said, rest assured that everyone that matters such as myself and Mr. Donahue is well aware of your background. He still decided to have you on board, so all your personal issues are no concern to your work and reputation. Now that that is out of the way. Off the record, what would you really like to talk about?"

"Strickland told me that he saw you while he was at your house with Ryan and Aniya. He said you played it cool as if you didn't just meet him earlier that day at the mall. I just want you to know that my son is a great young man who, for the most part, has been shielded from what happened to me. He does know that I went to prison, but as for the exact reason, we kept that from him. He doesn't know that Lance is his father, and since he's met Aniya he doesn't know that she's his sister. I do recall that you and Avery are friends, and I don't want my job to compromise your friendship with the two of you. I just wanted to be up front so there are no secrets on my end. As far as Kareem goes, we go way back and that's all it has been. We are just friends, nothing more, nothing less. I didn't even tell him who Lance was or that I was pregnant when I got into trouble, so he doesn't know anything either."

"Well, that's a lot to carry. Just know that your secret is safe with me and I'll do what I can to protect you. As long as you continue to be honest with me, we'll be fine. No worries. So, I'll end this conversation and pretend as if it never happened. I'll see you when you and Kupenda get here for the news I have to share."

"Thank you so much, that is indeed a relief. I truly appreciate you for allowing me to confide in you about my personal matters. I'll see you in a few minutes."

The call was disconnected.

Well I'll be damned. Ok, get it together girl. With all this going on, this poor child, Horisha, is really a casualty of Lance's bullshit. She truly has no idea as to what or who he really is. Now the question is, what do I do with this information? Do I tell Avery? Do I not say anything at all? If I keep quiet and it comes out that I know how all these pieces fit together I don't want to be at fault with someone being hurt. Ultimately that someone may be Avery and Aniya, but then again, Horisha and Strickland have no idea either.

As a matter of fact, I think I just figured out how to play all of this out. We need to have an open house to get everyone in the same place, so that it can all get put on the floor that Lance is the common denominator with all the fuckery that's going on.

Chapter 21

The Office

"Knock, knock, knock, we're all here Boss Lady. Are you ready for the meeting?"

"You know what? Yeah. I'm just putting away some of these documents for the house showings later today. Come on in. I'm ready."

Laughing and smiling is what I observed as everyone walked into the office. It was really nice to see them in work attire, looking all professional, myself included.

"Before I start this meeting, I want everyone to know that regardless of whatever happened before we all got to this moment, none of it matters. I truly have your best interest at heart, whether you believe me or not,"

As I looked directly in Kupenda's direction, "I just want you all to know that I am not your enemy. I have nothing but good intentions for each and every one of you. If you don't believe me, then ask Ronnie. Not only is he my assistant, but he's more like the daughter I never had."

As the ladies started laughing, Ronnie began to speak in a manly voice, "Boss Lady, you do realize that I'm a man?"

"I do, Ronnie. But when it comes to your flamboyant nature, I see so much of myself in you. Not to insult you, but you know you my girl."

"You got that shit right."

With a roll of the neck and a few snaps of his fingers he was back in Ronnie formation.

"Ok, y'all things are going much faster than I anticipated. I have to go meet with Mr. Donahue to get the papers to be signed, so I can officially change the game."

Ronnie interrupts, "What's going on Boss?"

"Well, if you let me finish, I ran into Mr. Donahue this morning. He told me that his last day at Keys Real Estate would be today. Effective tomorrow after I sign the papers today, I'll officially have Carrington & Associates on the marquee. That means this firm belongs to me. Since y'all work for me, I'm Carrington and you all are the associates. Granted there are other agents in the building, but who knows if they'll stay once they find out the changes that Mr. Donahue made for the future are indeed effective immediately. Needless to say, it's time to throw a party. Welcome aboard ladies, and gentlemen."

While everyone is smiling and a bit amazed by the news, I continue by telling them, "Horisha,

Kupenda, and Ronnie, I need you all to give me a list of 5 people you want to be here to celebrate your new positions. This will also serve as a meet and greet for all the new prospective clients. Technically, it's an open house for Carrington & Associates."

"All other issues we have we will take care of starting at the beginning of the week. But, our first order of business is to get the other colleagues together, so they can be aware of these new changes, and I'm sure Mr. Donahue has made all of them aware of the immediate changes.

Ronnie, I need you to create a social media press release about Carrington & Associates along with the updated housing list. Then, combine the two.

Horisha, I need you to go make sure your key cards and badges are printed out and working.

Kupenda, you my dear, get the menu together. You can have it catered, just call one of the restaurants in our Rolodex and decide what you think is best for the party. Please, nothing too fancy or anything too boring. Keep it at finger foods. Nothing to fill them up, just a light snack, and you also can order a cake. Does everyone have their missions?"

As Ronnie raised his hand, "Yes, Ronnie."

"When is this supposed to take place?"

"Oh, excuse me, I was thinking about Friday."

"You mean the day after tomorrow?"

"Yes. It will be in 2 days. Is that a problem?"

"Not at all, we are having a party on Friday, right before the weekend. Do we get champagne too?"

"You know what? That'll be fine. Get a case. We are about to celebrate a new beginning."

Before all this takes place, I need to contact Kareem and let him know to keep his calendar open for Friday. I don't want no shit with him. Besides I need him here, just in case some shit goes down, he'll be here to have my back. Then, I need to call Avery to let her know that I don't need her to get the building for me because of the recent changes of events. I got my own real estate agency, Carrington & Associates. I need to contact the printer, so I can get my name on the letterheads, envelopes, business cards, etc. Oh! How could I forget? I need a logo. Whoa! This is all happening way too fast. Let me slow down and take it one step at a time.

Back to Avery, what reason would she have to be here at the party on Friday? Hell, she's my friend, the mom of Aniya, who is Ryan's girlfriend. Hell, Lance is one of my biggest buyers. Well, that covers their invites. I guess now all I have to do is contact her and have her clear her schedule, so they'll be here on Friday. I need to make a hair and nail appointment. I also need to find something to wear. Maybe this was too soon, I should do it next week. But, no, I want Mr. Donahue to be able to be a part of the celebration and allow him to see the change over. This week it is.

As I take a few deep breaths, I pick up the phone to call Kareem, and as I'm picking up the phone, Ronnie lets me know that he's on line 4.

"Hey you! What's up? I was just about to call you. I wanted to let you know what has happened today at work. Before I do, is everything ok with you?"

"Oh yeah, I'm good. I'm just bending a few corners before I gotta get the boys from school. I can take them to the mall and pick up those shoes."

I ask, "Shoes, huh?"

Kareem responds, "Yeah. is there something else I should be grabbing?"

"No, I just love the way you take charge when it comes to me and the boys."

"Anyway, the reason I called you was to tell you Mr. Donahue is leaving today. As of tomorrow morning, I no longer work for Keys Real Estate. I am the owner of Carrington & Associates, so I'm throwing a party on Friday to introduce the new team and to let everyone know about the changes to the staff. While you're at the mall, can you get me something to wear? I need it to give boss, but sexy while also giving the I'm the shit vibes."

We both laughed on que.

"Dig that, I'm proud of you, little one. That's a big deal, say less. I got you covered. Just know, it ain't gone be solid black either."

"Well, you know my taste and I trust your judgement, so make your future wife look fly as fuck."

"Indeed. Well was that all you needed? To be honest, I didn't really want anything, but to remind you that I was getting the boys from school, so you won't be worried about them not being straight home. You know how you like to check those cameras."

As we both started laughing together, "I certainly appreciate that and that gives me some relief that you know how I feel about that. Thanks, babe."

"You got it, momma. I'll see you later tonight."

Chapter 22

Isis & Avery

The entire day was dedicated to switching stuff from Keys Real Estate to Carrington & Associates. I can't forget to call Avery and tell her to clear her schedule for Friday and kinda give her the heads up on what's going down up here. In fact Strickland is Lance's son, which would explain the strong facial features and his eyes. It's very rare to have one black one and one brown one. But in this case, can anything get any more strange?

Strickland meeting up with Ryan had to be simply coincidental. He truly doesn't know what's going on out here. All this baby knows is that his mother is home from prison. Anyway, that's another issue for another day, but not right now.

As I'm sitting in the office checking out the view of the city, I can't help but to be overjoyed with the elevation of my career and my life. It truly has been a journey getting here, but I'm grateful for all my trials.

I call out, "Ronnie."

"Yeah, Boss Lady, here I come."

While he's making his way, I want to be sure I express my gratitude because he's been here with me every step of the way, and I know without him I wouldn't be as successful as I am. He's a vital asset to this team.

"What's up? Do you need anything?"

"No, I just wanted to tell you how much I appreciate you and your work. You mean a lot to me and this team. I can't express that enough."

"Aww, Boss Lady, I too am grateful for you giving me the opportunity to show you how much of an asset I could be to the company."

He pauses with a bashful smile on his face.

Ronnie proceeds and says, "Are we over the mushy stuff? You know how easily you start crying and things."

In unison, we both started laughing together.

"Seriously, I want this congratulatory party to be epic, even though it's on such short notice of course."

"Oh yeah, you know I love planning parties on a budget."

"Excuse me, but who said we were on a budget? This is my opening party to let everyone know this is Carrington & Associates. We won't break the bank, but we will get it done on short notice."

"In that case, I got you. Before I start anything, what's the budget?"

"I don't have one, so just don't break the bank."

"Understood. I'll make you proud."

"As you always do. Thanks, Ronnie. Can you get Avery on line 4 please?"

"Got it. I'll let you know when she's on."

"Boss Lady, I got Avery."

"Avery, hey how's it going?"

"It's going as well as it can go for right now. I just feel like the walls are starting to close in on me. I got to finalize this deal on behalf of my father and I'm waiting for a location to meet up with the head of the organization. I've been thinking about the shit with Lance and his potential son. To be honest, it's weighing on my heart. What if he is Lance's son, which would mean that Aniya ain't the only child. What would that do to her financial future? I just don't know how to handle all these boomerangs life is throwing this way."

Taking a deep breath, I can only empathize with her because I really don't know what I would do if I was in that situation.

"I'm sorry to hear that. I'm sure it will all work out. Let's have you think about something else. On a different note, Mr. Donahue is leaving the agency today and he's turning it over to me. Beginning on Monday, it'll be Carrington & Associates. To commemorate the change, we are having a party on Friday to introduce the team to the other colleagues and introduce Carrington & Associates to the world. Will you and your family be my guests to the event?"

"Wow! Congratulations, that's a major deal. How do you feel about it? As far as the family coming, do you think it's a good idea considering his thot pockets are working for you?"

Laughing hysterically at the fact she used the words "thot pockets". It just tickled my spirit.

"Well if you decide not to come, considering all that's going on, I totally understand. I just wanted to extend the invitation to you because you're my friend. I don't want to share this without you being present. I won't push, but you are invited and I just wanted you to know."

"Wouldn't that be something to see Lance's face with all his hoes in one place?"

Speaking of hoes in one place, did you know he showed up at the Grey Bistro the other day? He was there alone and when he saw the two of them at our table, it was almost as if he saw two ghosts. He tried to play it cool. Girl, he stumbled over the chairs behind him as he walked away and everything. That shit was funny as hell."

"Naw, I didn't know. He must've spent cash because I didn't see any charges come across the statement. Was he there with anyone?"

"No, not that I could see. I said he was alone. He sat at the bar alone until we left anyway."

"Ok, well that's good. At least, I don't have more of his mistakes to worry about."

"Right. Oh, Avery, I also wanted to talk about one more thing.. As far as the prom goes, I have an idea. What do you think about having Ryan and Aniya along with some of their friends, a small gathering downstairs in the banquet hall? Considering the COVID restrictions, they can get dressed, wear masks, and practice social distancing. At least, we won't have to worry about where they are and we don't have to cover the cost for a building. Of course, we'll have to pay for a DJ, decorations, food, etc."

"Shit, girl, I think that's a great idea. I'll run it by Aniya and you talk to Ryan. We'll see how they feel about that and go from there. That's good shit and it will still let them have some sort of prom experience."

"Exactly! You know their moms are the shit. We just gotta show them we still got it. Let's show 'em what we working with."

As Avery continued to comment, "If I was right there, we'd be high fiving and taking shots."

"On that note, I'll wrap up this conversation and head out, so I can get some stuff done for Friday. Hope to see you, if not you at least I know I'll see Aniya because you know she ain't going nowhere without Ryan."

"You got that shit right. Keep me posted."

Now that Avery is out the way, or at least she knows about the party, hopefully she'll be able to make it. I don't want anyone to be uncomfortable, but hell everyday Lance keeps that little secret of his to himself it makes more people feel uneasy so to hell with him. Fuck him and his feelings.

I really hope this goes well and nothing off the wall happens. I'll have to have security there just in case. To be honest, Horisha and Kupenda look like they can throw them thangs, but the universe knows I don't want anything to happen on Friday. It's going to be a big day for me and the agency. So yeah enough of the negative thought waves, let me manifest some dope energy this way. The hope is everything will go off just as planned. I gotta blow this joint and catch the bank before they close.

KeanaMonique

Chapter 23

Lance Whitaker

Nothing feels better than walking into the bank and being called by your name. They value my business here and I love their customer service. Now that I've got the banking done for the business and my personal accounts, I know this party will be epic. I'm sparing no expense. This will be the grand opening of Carrington & Associates.

Leaving the bank, my cell phone rings and I don't know who it could be, but maybe it's a prospective buyer.

"Isis Carrington speaking. How can I be of assistance?"

The voice on the other end of the phone caused me to lose my breath, what the hell does he want?

"Isis, this is Lance and I need to talk to you. Can we meet somewhere?"

"Excuse me, but what do you want with me? No, we can't meet."

"Please, Isis. I'm sinking deeper and deeper. I don't have the money to pay Horisha. Last night, the story came on the news. Avery and Aniya were sitting there. Then, Aniya showed me a picture of Strickland

and asked me if there was something I needed to say. Like a punk ass coward, I told them no. It was not my finest hour."

"Hell, Lance, that was your exit to be honest with your family and you failed to take it. Since you lied, or hid the truth, what do you expect them to do when they find out the truth about your past secret? My granny used to say, 'What don't come out in the wash, it's coming out in the rinse.' The truth is coming out whether you like it or not. Before the shit hits the fan, you better come clean, and do it quickly."

"Isis, please I need to talk to you. Where are you? Can I meet you, please?"

"Lance, that's not a good idea. Furthermore, please don't call me again."

"Isis, please, I'm desperate."

"What do you think I can do to help you? This is way beyond my scope of practice. I already told you what I think you should do, so I am at a loss for what you think I can help you with?"

"I just got off the phone with Avery, and she told me about the party on Friday, and I'm begging you, please cancel it. I need more time to figure this out."

"Cancel my party? Hell naw, you gotta be out yo' fucking mind. The audacity of you to even ask me something like that in an attempt to save your own ass. Get the fuck outta here with that bullshit. Get off my phone."

"Isis, please, I'm desperate. I'm begging you."

"Bye, nigga."

The nerve of this muthafucka to call and ask me to cancel my event because he doesn't want his business all out. It's too late, nigga. The cat is out the bag and who gives a fuck? You just have no idea what the fuck you just did. Game on, nigga.

Pick up the phone, Kareem. Come on. Pick up. As the phone is ringing, I'm getting irritated with each ring and I can't take it.

Kareem answers, "Yo', what's good, ma?"

As I started to tell him what's wrong, I let my emotions get the best of me and what did I do that for? Before I knew it, I started to cry. I don't cry. I'm a pretty thug, and thugs don't cry.

"Slow down, what the fuck is going on? Why the hell are you crying? Where are you?"

“You know how I just told you about the party on Friday, well I told Avery too. Apparently, Avery told Lance.”

“Ok. So, what's wrong with that?”

“Everything. Horisha, Kupenda, Avery, and Strickland will all be there.”

“Still not following. Come on, hit me with the shit.”

“Lance just calls me talking about how he wants me to cancel the party because he is not ready to face his past. Like what the fuck? The audacity for him to even call me and think that it would be ok to ask that. I can’t believe he would do that shit to me. His wife is my friend and I don’t owe him shit.”

“Are you done? If not, then you should be. That nigga just didn’t tie up his loose ends and now he’s expecting you to help him do that shit for him. Have the party, enjoy yourself, fuck that nigga, and let the shit hit the fan. Go get in the car, wipe your face and head to the crib.”

As I’m walking to the car, wiping my tears, and gathering myself, I reply, “I still have another stop to make, then I’ll be home. What time are you getting there?”

"I'm already here with the boys. Take your time. We'll be here."

"Ok. I'll be there as soon as I finish up."

I can't believe him. Lance has totally lost his mind. I can't wait until this shit blows up in his face and just for his shenanigans I just can't wait to see when he gets everything he deserves. He definitely tried the right one. I'm Isis Muthafuckin' Carrington!

Chapter 24

Nothing like Home

It's so good to be home. I just want to have some quiet time with the family, and of course some dick. I can't believe the day I just had. It actually went from sugar to shit in less than 24 hours.

Walking through the door, it's time to put my mommy hat on, cut this phone off and toss it in my purse. I'm so over work and everybody outside these four walls. Fuck outside.

"Mommy, mommy, guess what I got?" Dino says.

I swear nothing makes my day more than this right here. I love coming home and seeing my children.

"What do you have baby?I got my spelling test and I missed one word, but I still got an A. But, it's an A-."

As much joy as he had on his face for his spelling test was enough to erase all the trauma of my own day.

"Well, that's amazing, baby. Let's put it right on the refrigerator just like we said earlier."

Grabbing the tape out the kitchen drawer and getting ready to place it on the refrigerator, Dino yells out, "Look at my shoes, mommy, I just love these. They're my favorite color, blue."

"Wow! I love those. Looks like your feet are getting big, just like you. Soon you'll be tall like Ryan."

I swear the innocence of a child is enough to warm the coldest heart.

"So, Ryan, I'm unsure if you talked to Aniya about the prom issue, but I spoke with Avery. We had a bomb suggestion. We could rent out the ballroom at the office. The two of you could have some friends from school and we have a small version of y'all prom there. We'll decorate, have food, and play music too. Nothing too big, but at least, it'll be something for you all to remember for your senior year. What do you think of that?"

"Man, I think that's a great idea. I'm game. I'll let the homies know what's up and I'll get you a list of people before the weekend. I swear you always know how to pull blood from a turnip."

Laughing slightly, I replied, "If I didn't know any better, I'd swear you sounded like your Mimi."

With a suave look on his face, he said, "You know it. That's my Mimi."

Looking over to the den, I spoke to Kareem.

"Hey, babe, are you alright over there?"

"Oh yeah, Ma, I'm good. I'm just looking over some of these contracts that Sinclair Roman sent over about the deal. You need something?"

Looking at him with that look in my eyes, "After the day I had I need something only you can provide."

He looked at me and simply said, "Indeed. Me too."

We both knew what that meant. Once the children go to bed, it was definitely going to be adult time. It's about to go down.

An enjoyable evening eating dinner, conversing with the family, and just reconnecting with them while maintaining whatever it is that makes us unique. I love my family and it's perfect. Sometimes I wish I had a daughter, but who wants to do it all over again?. I'm well situated in my career and the boys are coming into their own individualities so why would I shake things up with a baby? Aniya is enough to give me that fix I need every now and again. So with all that being said, my family is perfect.

“Who’s cleaning the kitchen? Don’t all volunteer at once?”

“I gotta study.” Ryan yelled out.

Dino said, “I’m too short to do the dishes.”

Smiling from ear to ear, I said, “Well, that only leaves one person, Kareem. You got kitchen duty.”

Before he could debate it, I said, “I’m going to take a shower and I’ll see you when you finish the dishes.”

I winked and everyone left the table and went to do their own thing.

In my bedroom, I started the shower and grabbed my bed clothes, as if I’m going to need those. Laughing to myself, I immediately thought of the bathroom incident. I don’t know why I keep thinking about him. I swear he showed me something and it’s really making me wonder why I ghosted him. I’m glad I did because of the connection to De’Angelo, but hey that little nigga got it going on. Whoever he gets with is going to be extremely satisfied in that department.

While I’m in the shower, I hear the door open and Kareem walks in.

He asks, “Do you need your back washed?”

Turning around exposing my birthday suit, I told him, "A shower wouldn't be complete, if my back wasn't washed."

I invited him in to join me. Now when he offered to wash my back, I assumed it was with a washcloth, but instead I got an oral washing. Kisses so gentle and his hands were rubbing up and down my back. All I could do was stand there. Let the water hit my breast and enjoy the moment. As he continued to saturate my back with kisses, his hands had other plans. Massaging my soaking wet breast ever so gently and every now and then a gentle squeeze on my nipples just aroused me to the point where I wanted to instantly have shower sex. But, I was able to maintain my composure and let him take control. Lately, he's been acting strange talking about all that marriage stuff, and with him being so calculated I couldn't help but to be anxious about his next move.

Speaking of moves, we moved from the shower to the bed. Instead of jumping right into love making, he oiled me up. Every inch of me, from the top of my head to the soles of my feet. He massaged me and kissed me at the same time. Maybe it's me but, this is different for him. He's more passionate. He's connecting with me on every level. I mean, we have connected mentally, emotionally, and of course, physically.

He turned me over and began to kiss me. The sweetest ever forehead kiss has to be the most endearing, intimate moment ever. From my forehead to my nose, both cheeks then he looked me in my eyes and kissed me so passionately. I swear I felt my juice box start to pulsate. As he kissed me, his hands took another lead and walked all over my body, with his tongue to follow. There was something about the way he was into me this time. It wasn't like the times before. His energy was amazing. His vibe on smooth and the frequency was tuned to a perfect pitch. The tricks he was doing with his tongue put me on another level.

As he made his way down to my love below, he gently bit my inner thighs and ran his hands down the small of my back to assist me in arching it to a perfect position, so he could partake in dessert. He parted my freshly waxed pleasure palace and proceeded to enjoy every inch of me.

Slightly moaning in pleasure, he looked up at me and told me to hold it, and not to release the juice until he was ready to swallow every drop of fluid that came out of my body. Obediently. I did what I was told. He began to insert two fingers and used the come here motion inside me, teasing my G-spot. That alone increased the depth of passion that I was experiencing. It was almost as if he was down there at the palace for a record-breaking time, but the minute I was getting ready to release. He stopped.

He climbed on top of me and said, "You know everything I do for you is to add to your happiness, and you add to me just by being who you are. I've known you for over half your life and I've watched you grow. It's scary how much you act like me, think like me, and speak like me at times. I just wanted you to know how much I care about you and the boys. Nothing or nobody else will do it for me. Can I have you?"

I replied, "You already got me."

He kissed me again and said, "That's my girl."

He never said another verbal word, but his body spoke a language that made so much sense. It was almost as if our bodies were talking to each other. After he inserted his pleasure pole inside my pleasure palace, we both moaned in sexual bliss. Our bodies had a rhythm so undeniable you couldn't tell who was who.

This sexual exchange of energy was amazing. He was the perfect fit. This time it wasn't too rough. It wasn't too fast paced. It was perfect. As he kept the flow going, so did my waterfall, every thrust, I released just the right amount of juice to keep the wet. It was almost as if my body knew what to do. I've never had to think about not being wet when it came to him because he knew exactly what to do with my body.

We both are digging into each other's skin with just the right amount of passion. Moans exchanged equally. If that wasn't good enough, he must have known that I was getting ready to climax because he suddenly slid out of me. He put his face in the palace and told me to release everything that was bottled up, because he was ready to swallow. He reinserted his fingers to massage my G-spot and as he was going in and out with his fingers, his tongue started to circle my clitoris clockwise, then counter clockwise. Before I knew it, I released everything that I had been holding on to.

As he welcomed the liquid facial, he was licking and slurping every drop of juice I had released. He added a bit of pressure on my lower abdomen to help release the rest of what was inside. I was completely satisfied, but yet that was only the beginning. After that, he did what I was expecting, just the right amount of roughness. He flipped me over, arched my back, and began to give those long deep strokes.

Stroking in and out, out and in, he started to gently pull my hair, with a few ass smacks, a few gentle scratches, and he leaned over to whisper in my ear, and said, "Will you have me?"

In a passionate response I said, "Yes."

He asked again, and I replied the same thing.

And the third time he asked, I could tell that his body was about to release itself, and before I knew it, he exhaled.

He laid down and played in my hair, and he said, "Don't move. Stay right where you are."

I relaxed, took a deep breath, and that was the perfect ending of a topsy-turvy type of day. As we're laying there entangled in one another, it was at that moment, I realized that he was still inside me.

Chapter 25

The Day Before

The best part of waking up, is not giving a fuck. You know, that'll be my motto for the day. Yesterday was a bit uneasy and things were kind of shaky, but today is a new day and everything will be better than the day before.

Rolling out of bed, doing the usual, and making sure everyone is good, but today, there's a different type of vibe in the house. Could it be that I don't give a fuck today? Could it be that something is off with Kareem? Whew, chile, last night, I don't know who that was, but whoever it was, he needs to stick around. My boys are great. However, I can't put my finger on the awkwardness of this energy. I do know one thing. I'll be damned if it stops me or anything that has to do with tomorrow's event.

Where's my purse? Wherever the purse is, therein lies my cell phone. It was so peaceful last night without it. I think I'll have to do that more often. I will just take a pause on technology. I had a great evening with the family. Now, let me see what bullshit I've missed.

To my surprise, my cell phone is absolutely dry. Not one call, not one text, nothing. I can't believe that. I know something had to take place, and if it did, and I don't know anything about it, then that means it has nothing to do with me. But, hell, if it didn't have anything to do with me, then nobody thought enough of me to spill the tea.

"Good morning, babies! Did you all get some rest?"

Dino's cheerful voice replied, "Yes, I did. But, I kept hearing Ryan talking to Aniya on the phone, all mushy-mushy."

Dino makes a kissy face to make fun of Ryan.

Ryan snaps, "You don't know what you're talking about. It wasn't all mushy-mushy. Shut up and eat, so we can go."

"Hey, hey, now, is everything alright with you Ryan? You seem a bit edgy."

"Yeah, Ma, I'm good. I just had a slight disagreement with Aniya last night about the dude, Strickland. He slid in her DMs."

"Whoa! Strickland?"

"Yeah, she said all he did was ask her who was cool to hang around with, but, hell, he could've asked me that. You told me to protect her and that's what I'm trying to do. But, she thinks I'm doing too much. So, yeah, we kinda beefin'. But, she'll be outside in a few to get us for school."

"You know what? Baby, just drive my car. I'll have Kareem take me to work and you can pick me up. One thing for sure is you don't ever want anyone to think they gotta do shit for you. That goes for anybody, and I do mean anybody."

Leaning towards him, I hugged him, fixed his shirt, and gave him a kiss. I handed him my keys and sent him on his way.

Turning around to go get dressed for work, I passed Kareem on his way trying to leave.

"Wait! Where are you going? I need a ride to work."

"I gotta make a move really quick. How long will it be before you get ready? I'll wait."

"Well, give me 20 minutes and I'll be ready."

"I tell you what, take them 20 minutes, get ready, and I'll be back. Then, you can drop me off."

He kissed me and left.

Standing there with a twisted look on my face, 'drop me off 'were the words that were on repeat in my mind. Yeah, I knew something wasn't right this morning because when has he ever said drop me off. Yeah, let me get my sage and start cleansing my aura because something ain't right. Let me get my ass ready. I got 18 minutes because I know he is punctual.

Just as I was finishing getting ready and completing my final look, I must admit this YSL wrap around dress looks amazing on me, if I do say so myself. I swear he has perfect timing.

As I was opening the door, he opened it, and said, “Damn, you got perfect timing. I said 20 minutes and you're looking real sexy to be the soon-to-be Mrs. Kareem Anderson.”

“Mrs. Kareem Anderson? Wow, you talking real slick about that marriage stuff. Oh, don’t think I didn’t realize that you did not pull-out last night. Talking about ‘don’t move, stay right there.’”

As he laughed and said, “Quit trippin’. You know you wanna have my daughter, since ain’t no little girl running around here.”

Playfully pushing him, “Boy, ain’t nobody trying to have no baby right now. Let’s go. I gotta get to work.”

Driving down the street listening to one of his CDs, it had a smooth beat and the flow was nice. I gotta admit, he got skills. Yes, that's my baby.

Kareem put his hand on my leg and looked at me and said, “You know what? I’m proud of you.

Living out your dream, I can't wait to see what you have up your sleeve for tomorrow."

"Well, you won't get a sneak peek about it. I guess you'll just have to be there to find out."

"I already cleared my schedule, so I can be there to support you. I wouldn't miss it for the world."

"Also, I want to thank you for keeping your word and taking Dino to get his shoes. You really made his day."

"That's my lil homie. I'll do anything for those fellas. I love them like they were my own."

As he was finishing up, he was making it to his destination, which was about 15 minutes away from my job, and actually it's right in the area of where Ronnie lives.

"Who lives over in this area?"

"Sinclair Roman. We need to chop it up about these contracts and make sure everything is legit. Not that I doubt him, but you know I ain't never too sure. I always gotta make sure the i's are dotted and the t's are crossed. Give me a kiss."

We kissed so passionately and it made me think of last night. It got me all moist.

Licking my lips, I said to him, “I'll see you later. Do you need me to pick you up?”

“Naw, I'll get a ride to the crib.”

“To the crib?”, I repeated sarcastically.

“You heard what I said. Now, gone head and get to work. I'll call you and check on you later.”

Leaving the area, I might as well call Ronnie and see what's up.

“Ronnie, I'm so glad you answered. You good?”

“Yeah. I'm chillin'. You good, Boss Lady?”

“Oh, you know me. I'm always Gucci. Do you need a ride to work or are you already in transit?”

“A ride? You do know I stay out of your way. I'm good though. I'm about to pull up to the office.”

“Alright, well, I'll see you in about 15 minutes.”

Ronnie's temperature is good, but I still can't help but to think why do I still have this eerie feeling that's trying to overtake me. However, in true fashion, I'll see exactly what I need to see. Trying to shake and move, I'm trying to get my vibe right for the day. I couldn't help but to do a quick overview of the possible list of things to do to get ready for tomorrow. I know the paperwork with HR is handled, the logo has been submitted, and everything thus far is ready for the switch from Keys Real Estate to Carrington & Associates. I can't believe this is happening to me in such a short time. Well, I'm ready to take on the responsibility of the new position.

Approaching the office, there seems to be some commotion in the parking lot. Let me hurry up and see what appears to be the problem. I swear I don't want to have any issues right before I take over. This better not be nothing that has anything to do with me or my team.

All I hear is yelling. Now, that's one red flag. There won't be any yelling on these grounds. I refuse to have the new home of Carrington & Associates known as a breeding ground for drama. The closer I get to the building the clearer the scene gets. I know, damn well, this ain't who I think it is. What in the entire fuck is De'Angelo doing back up here? Wait a minute, is that Lance too?. As I do another quick scan of the parking lot, I also see Horisha, Kupenda, and Ronnie. The last person to arrive would be me, so let's figure this shit out.

Hurrying to get my things and get to the middle of the bullshit, I can't help but to try to quickly put all the pieces together in my head. De'Angelo is still mad at Ronnie. Lance is livid about the payout with Horisha, but I can't figure out what that has to do with this, besides the fact that he ain't fucking with her no more. Shaking my thoughts around, let's calm this down before someone calls security and we all lose our jobs.

"Hey, hey, hey, what is going on? Why is everybody all out here in front of the building yelling and acting like we don't have the sense we were born with? Ronnie, answer me what's going on?"

Pulling him away from the commotion to separate the parties, I grabbed Horisha and told her to get Kupenda and head up to the office now.

"Ronnie, look at me. What the fuck is going on?"

Visibly upset, Ronnie attempts to tell me what he observed when he walked up.

"Ok, look when I was parking the car, I noticed Lance was talking with Kupenda. From what I could tell, it was getting a bit heated because she started talking with her hands. So, I knew from the conversation and hand motions that some shit was about to go down. So, when I was running up, I saw Horisha running too. Then, it wasn't about Kupenda no more 'cause Horisha started asking him where her money was. They started going back and forth, so I'm trying to calm them down. Then, out of nowhere comes De'Angelo talking about how he can't get a job and it's all my fault 'cause of what went down at the wedding. You know I was defending myself and it got heated. I think security was called, and then you showed up."

Taking it all in, all I could think was what the hell?

"Are you sure that's all De'Angelo was saying?"

Ronnie replied with a short snappy comeback, "Yes! Toilet Tina, he didn't mention his nephew."

As relieved as I was for that little bit of information, I tried not to seem insensitive towards the situation.

All I could say was, "Shut up. I'm trying to figure out a spin on this, so if and when security shows up I'll know what to say. Those two bastards came up here on some bullshit, so I need to cover my employees at all costs. So save me the dramatics, please."

Let's go inside and check on the girls.

Entering the building, I knew the shit was already among the others, because here comes Mr. Donahue and security.

"Good morning, Mr. Donahue, I have settled everything outside and as of right now all is well."

In my attempts to smooth things over before, it gets worse.

"Good morning, Isis. After I survey this mess out here, I need to see you in my office, so head there right now. Thank you."

He kept walking. I swear this day can't get any worse. I knew from the time I got up that something was uncomfortable about this day. Sure as shit, it gets crazier by the minute.

"Ok, Ronnie, I need to see what the fuck he knows or doesn't know. Go get yourself together and check on the girls. We'll brief each other when I return."

He just gave me a head nod and we parted ways.

Sitting here waiting on Mr. Donahue, it's almost like time has completely stopped. It felt like an eternity because it's not that far of a walk, nor was it that much to assess. This is going to hell in a handbasket. I have to think of a way to spin this in my favor. I can't have him second guessing his choice to leave the company to me.

The minute I think I got it down to a reasonable solution in walks Mr. Donahue.

"What a way to start the morning, don't you agree?," says Mr. Donahue, with the most sarcastic tone known to man.

"I, most certainly do. I was just pulling myself up when I saw the minor melee. But enough of all that, please just give it to me straight."

As he took a deep breath in, I just knew I was about to lose a job before I even got it for real.

"For starters, you know I value you and the team that you're building, but this is the second time this DeAngelo man has come up here starting things with Ronnie. Now, I don't want to assume but, is there something going on with Ronnie that's causing this man to continue to come up here and be a nuisance at his place of employment? I'm not accusing him. I'm just trying to leave this company in the hands of someone who won't run it into the ground. I'm not saying you will, but it could be the company you keep, so before I tell you to fire him, I'm going to let you know this will not happen again."

I'm listening and trying not to look stressed. Mr. Donahue continues.

"Although I am leaving the company, you will be on a probationary period for 3 months and after you've completed that period, then the company will officially be yours. It's all in the documents, but in case you or someone on your team messes up, your contract is terminated. Do I make myself clear?"

"I understand. Just so we're clear, my contract for the new position starts on Monday of this upcoming week. Is that right?"

Looking at the calendar, Mr. Donahue says, "Yes, it starts Monday and my last day was supposed to be yesterday, but I'll be here until tomorrow. I don't want to miss your party. The party will be well controlled, right?"

Looking at him with a slight side eye, "Yes and it will have added security, just in case."

I added a wink and hopefully that was enough to get me out of the hot seat.

"Will that be all?," I asked.

"Yes, it is, Isis, thank you and I know you won't let me down. I'll talk to you later on today. Don't forgct about what I said. Shape the ship up or everybody is shipping out."

"Yes, Mr. Donahue."

I took a deep breath as I walked out of his office and prepared for my walk of shame.

Chapter 26

The Aftermath

Walking back to the office, I see my colleagues looking out their office windows or staring over their coffee cups at me like I did something wrong. I can't wait to run this shit, so I can fire their asses. But for now let me get my nice girl on, they already think I'm young black and immature anyway.

All fun and games aside, this shit is totally unbalanced. Mr. Donahue thinks all this bullshit has to do with Ronnie and Ronnie wasn't even initially here for the nonsense. I gotta talk with my team. We can't let them think that giving the company to me was the wrong move. Toughen up girl, you got some fish to fry and this grease is hot as fuck. So this is all just another piece of the pie, I got to cut into before tomorrow. I don't know if things are going to work out. It's just too much and I'm getting scared. Granny, if you're listening, please show and tell me what to do. I need to know what to do, so I won't lose my job. I need my team members to keep theirs as well. We gotta make it until 5pm tomorrow or at least until the party is over.

Entering my office, I can't help but admire the view. Also, considering if I don't get this shit together this might be my last time looking at this view.

Laughing and saying to myself, I'm Isis Muthafuckin' Carrington and ain't no nigga or anybody for that matter getting ready to take me from somewhere I worked so hard to get to.

"Ronnie, this rabbit hole goes a bit deeper than I thought. What's up with the girls?"

Smacking his lips, rolling his hips, and before he put that finger in the air, I cut his ass off.

"Listen, I know you're pissed, but now isn't the time for the venting session. We'll do that later on after work. We'll go to the bar for drinks and talk, but right now it's business, please."

"Boss Lady, I don't know what the heck I gotta do with De'Angelo not being able to get a job, but he can't keep coming up here messing with me. I'm contacting the detective and letting him know what went down this morning. Hopefully, I can get this resolved. This is insane."

"Well, that sounds very productive and I'm proud of your response. Before you contact the police, tell me about the girls."

In true Ronnie fashion, he just can't help himself when he's upset, he smacks those lips like nobody's business.

"I think Horisha got it under control, but she kept mentioning something about the 50 Gs that he owes her. She reminded him he needs to pay up before she air his shit out."

" Now what shit is she talking about airing out exactly?"

Ronnie admits, "I don't know, but it can't be good because when she said that to him, he straightened up real quick. He didn't say anything else really. But, Kupenda is a different story. He was harassing her about not calling him back and he was on that Suga zaddy shit with her., but that bread done got stale and so did he."

Thinking, damn that's a lot to take in, but I think I got it.

"Have them meet me down here, so we can corroborate our stories."

"But, why if that's the truth?"

"Because these white walls have eyes and ears, and just because we say it happened one way doesn't mean that's the way they saw it or heard it."

"You're right. I'll be back shortly."

I have to call Kareem and let him know what just happened. This shit is crazy. Before I call him, let me send Avery a message. I don't know when she's supposed to meet with the people from the organization as she so eloquently put it. Laughing to myself. Hopefully, she'll be here tomorrow for the party. Snapping out of my daze, my team walks in.

Taking a mafia stance and trying to keep a straight face, I asked who wanted to start talking first. Kupenda surprisingly started talking.

Kupenda starts, "I'll go first, since I was the first one here. I was standing outside the door just waiting a few more minutes before I decided to come in and work. I was standing there messing with my phone. Then, I hear Lance say, 'Damn, baby you don't know how to call me no more?' Before I knew it and remembered I was at work, I snapped. I went from A to Z on that nigga. I went off on his ass about me losing the condo, all his lies, him fucking with Nunuu, and all that shit. By the time I realized it, here comes Horisha.

" Horisha, do you want to follow up?"

Horisha continues the story, "Indeed, I do. When I get out of the car all I see is Kupenda hands up in the air like she is about to start windmilling somebody. I started running over there to see what was up, and when I realized it was Lance, I couldn't help myself. I asked him where my fucking money was at. When he saw me push Kupenda out the way, he knew it was game time. Instead of him jumping at me, he thought twice and I told him to remember that I got his balls in my hands. He better act right. He proceeded to walk away. After that, all I heard was Ronnie yelling at De'Angelo. I, honestly, don't even know when he came up here.

I look at Ronnie and say, "Last, but not least, Ronnie you wanna take the floor?"

He, then, starts his portion of the story.

"Yeah. When I saw them two yelling and stuff, I ran over to see what was up with them. De'Angelo popped up out of nowhere. He was talking about that mess like I'm the reason he can't get a job because of that wedding mess. I was trying to blow him off and get us all in the building. Then, you pulled up. That's it. That's all, nothing more and nothing less."

"Well, I'll be damned. Ok, that's a lot. Well, just to let y'all know all at once, we are all on probation and if one more situation happens like this, we're all gone. Mr. Donahue pulled me into his office this morning and gave me the business. Y'all, come on. Let's keep it professional up here. I'm not saying y'all did anything wrong, but we are the pepper in the salt around here. Let's not give them any more reasons to talk shit about us. Agreed?"

Everybody agreed and we went on about our business.

"Horisha, let me talk to you before you leave out please."

"Should I pull up a chair or continue to stand?" She asks.

"Either one you do is fine. So about this money, you do know there are other ways to get it instead of popping off at your place of employment. You do know you're still on papers and anything can get you flagged."

"I know and I'm sorry. I just snapped when I saw him talking shit to Kupenda, but you're right. I'll be more professional. Will you be calling my PO?"

"I won't, but you might want to give the heads up in case someone from the higher ups calls."

"That's a good idea! I'm on it right now. Thank you so much. I'll email you our guest list for tomorrow's party. Between Kupenda and myself, it's only 5 including us."

"Sounds perfect, thanks. That'll be all. Please close my door on the way out."

Exhaling loudly, I swear I want to scream, but shit my team is solid. Their stories all matched

Ronnie's, so I'm going to war for mine. Those other two idiots got to get what's coming to them. This can't happen again, especially once it becomes Carrington & Associates. Reaching over the desk to get my cell phone to send Avery a message, I notice that she's already sent me one.

The text reads, "I gotta fly out to California this morning for the meeting. I should be back tonight. I'll text you when I touch down, and give you all the hotel information. Nobody knows I'm gone but you. Again, I'll be back tonight."

What the entire fuck? She just left by herself. I'm over today already, and it's only 10:17am. Ok, now Kareem, you're up next. I call and he actually answers on the second ring.

"What's up? Baby, you good?"

"Hell naw, De'Angelo came up to the job..."

Before I could finish, he interrupted me and was like, "That nigga, don't get it. I thought I made myself perfectly clear, apparently not."

As he took a deep breath, he told me not to worry about him and that he would handle the scandal. When that man talks to me in the frequency that only he can, I just be wanting to jump his bones through the phone.

"Well if you say so,"

"Don't doubt what I said. I said I'll handle it."

"No shade, but you told me that once before."

If I didn't know any better, I'd think he was getting a bit aggravated with me not believing him about handling the shit. But, I'm just speaking facts right now. With so much passion in his voice, I could've easily mistaken it for aggression, but since I know him. I let it slide.

"I got it. For the record, I got you and in 24 years I've never let you down. I won't start slippin' now. I got it."

The phone went dead.

Did this nigga just hang up on me? Naw, the signal faded at just the right time. Yeah, that's what happened. I'll let that one slide. As a matter of fact, I need to let it slide, because he's not my issue. If I call him back, then I'll only bc taking my negative energy out on him and that's not cool. Let me go walk it off and drink some water because this day is for the birds already.

"Ronnie, I need to get some air. I'll be back, take any messages, and don't forget to contact the people you're supposed to be calling."

He held up the phone to let me know he was on the phone with them at that very moment. I winked and walked away.

Walking down the hall, I get to the elevators and apparently bad news travels fast as fuck because some of my colleagues are all at the water cooler snickering and side eyeing me. All I can think is well, keep it up because in three months, this muthafucka is all mine and I'm shitting on y'all severance checks. That is if y'all get one at all. Being me, I waved and blew kisses to let them know I was on to their ass. What a quick way to disperse because that sure as shit did the trick.

I'm taking the stairs. I need to get some of this energy off me anyway. I look too damn sexy to not run this company. I gotta get this shit under control. Once I made it outside, I just leaned up against the building. I took a few deep breaths in through the nose and out the mouth. I have to shake this shit because it's been on me since I woke up this morning. Attempting to relax, I notice that Mr. Donahue has immediately increased security. They're all up and through the parking lot. All of a sudden, as I was leaning on the building, on the left of me, I saw the most beautiful blue robin. I've always loved birds. Whenever I need peace on any matter, robins always calm me. They let me know that everything will be just fine.

With a new found energy I go back inside to confirm the details for tomorrow.

"Ronnie, is everything alright with that particular situation?"

"Yes, Boss Lady, the detective is on it and handling it. He said he'll be in touch."

"Fine, that's wonderful news. As far as tomorrow goes, did you confirm with the decorator, caterer, and the guest list?"

"Already done. The press release is on your desk also and ready for you to proofread. The social media flier is in your email, awaiting your approval, as well. I'm two steps ahead of you."

"You are indeed a fantastic aide to me and this firm. What a jewel you are. I'll be in my office if you need anything."

While at my desk admiring the view of the city, I can't help but to think of Avery's safety. I can't wait to speak with her to confirm she made it safe and to let her know of Lance's fuckery at the office today. Not to mention how De'Angelo made a complete asshole of himself, coming up here blaming Ronnie for his inability to secure employment.

"Ronnie, do we have any showings this afternoon? I've got to get out of this office."

"There's actually two appointments that are scheduled. Should I call and confirm?"

"Bring me the listings and confirm."

Well now, I actually should send out Horisha to do the showing, but I'll shadow her before I throw her to the wolves. With a sarcastic grin on my face, I think that will be just fine. While we're gone, Ronnie can train Kupenda on a few things.

"Ronnie, can you call down to Horisha's office and let her know that she'll be joining me to do the showing of this house this afternoon. While we're gone, you and Kupenda can do some training."

"Boss Lady, that sounds like a plan. I'll show her how to properly file the client's information and I'll think of some other stuff."

"That's good. We got 90 days to show and prove, and I'm not about to mess up this opportunity. Let me know when Horisha's ready, so we can head out."

If Horisha has as much heart for real estate as she shows for the streets, then she'll do just fine. I see a lot of myself in her. Let me get my head back in the game before I become the game and get played.

I'm Isis Muthafuckin' Carrington, and this is what I do. I sell houses. I sell property. I sell future goals. Oh my goodness! that's it. That's the new firm's slogan. 'Here at Carrington & Associates, we not only sell houses, we sell affordability. Realistic dreams at a fraction of the cost.'

Now that I'm saying it out my mouth, it still needs some work. Doodling while waiting on Horisha, I decided to fix myself some tea. I prefer Chamomile Raspberry by HiddenRaham. It is my absolute favorite. It's light, fresh, and it doesn't have a nasty aftertaste. As I'm sipping, gazing and waiting, Horisha walks in.

"I heard you want to take me out and show me the ropes." She said jokingly.

"Yeah, that sounds about right. I would feel horrible just throwing you to the wolves. You know that's not the right way to do things. But just for shits and giggles, I would like to see how you act. As a matter of fact, the first showing will be mine, and the next one you're on your own. Trust me, that's doing a lot because Mr. Donahue just told me to meet a prospective buyer at whatever address and come back with a purchase agreement. Talk about wolf throwing."

We both laughed as we hurried out to the car for our house selling outing.

Horisha starts to speak, but appears to be apprehensive. "Isis, do you think I'll make a good real estate agent?"

Stunned by her question, I reply, "Why would you think otherwise? This is what you want to do with your life, right?"

"Of course, but with me just coming home and being a fresh face around here, it's not easy to win over the majority just by being a fresh face."

"I understand your concern and when you know the ABC's it makes it easier for you to seal the deal."

"The ABCs of real estate?" Horisha questioned.

"Exactly, A- Always B- Be C- Closing. No matter what they say they need, you already got it. They have kids, then you have the perfect daycare or latch key program. They like the landscaping, but they can't grow flowers. Then, you have a botanical buddy on speed dial. They look parched, then pass them water. I'm sure you get my point. ALWAYS BE CLOSING. Never let them second guess the decision they've made. You will be their first impression of their new home, their new potential family foundation. It's you. They will never forget you, and your willingness to go the extra mile. Once you've made them feel secure in their decision, rest assured that they will continue to talk about your efforts and pass the word. This will bring you more clients. As always, more clients, more responsibility and overall more money. Got it?"

Smiling so securely, she replied, "I most certainly do. Thank you so much."

Giving her the wink of approval, I pushed her slightly and said, "Now, let's go show the new prospective buyer how well we know our ABCs."

Chapter 27

The Office

As we excitedly made our way back to the office, I was so impressed with Horisha's performance. We will return victorious with two purchase agreements in hand. I turned to Horsiha to congratulate her on her outstanding performance on her first day at selling houses. She looks so happy that she was able to seal two deals, and if I didn't know any better I'd say she almost had me beat. But, hell I do this. I've taught her everything she knows. But, I didn't teach her everything I know. She's not my competition. She's my protégé. She is a damn good one, might I add.

Horisha looked at me and said, "Isis, I want to thank you for believing in me and taking me under your wing in this business. Most importantly, I thank you for keeping my secret. I truly appreciate you."

"My pleasure, Horisha, it is indeed my pleasure to equip you with everything you need to be successful in your future endeavors. Now let us go and see what trouble the two of our assistants have gotten into."

"Hopefully, none." Horisha added.

Walking into the office, I can slightly hear some music coming from my office. I know good and well Ronnie ain't up in here acting a fool while I'm gone. He knows good and well we are already under a microscope.

"Excuse me, Ronnie, what do you think you're doing? That music is entirely too loud, I can hear it approaching the office."

Looking as if nothing was wrong, he looked at me and said, "That's not coming from this office. Don't you think I know better. It's coming from Mr. Donahue's office. He said he wanted to lighten the mood around here. Word has spread about his cancer returning and he didn't want to feel down about it. He also mentioned that he wanted to keep his spirits up over the next day or so, so the office would be a place of positive energy. He wants to leave on a bright note."

Surprisingly, I couldn't do anything but smile. If it's positive energy he wants, then that's what he'll get.

"So, Ronnie, enlighten me on the training of Kupenda, how did that go?"

"Actually, she's picking up things much faster than I anticipated. She catches on fast, and she has done quite well. We went over the client form prep, the filing system, email and social media blasts. How did the showings go?"

"Now, you know the ABCs always work. We have two purchase agreements to follow up on. This is something else she needs to know, so you go and work on that with her. Here's the information you need. Do I have any phone calls that need to be returned?"

"No, but you left your cell phone on your desk and it's been blowing up."

"The fuck? How could I do something like that? I, honestly, didn't miss it. Shit, let me go and see what is going on."

Checking my cell phone, my heart is beating faster than usual. I just hope all is well and I haven't missed anything that requires my immediate attention. Checking my phone, and all I could do was take a deep breath. It's nothing to worry about. I'll return these calls later. My children are good and Kareem is still working. However, I can't stop to think about Avery, and I know that plane has landed. I pray she's ok. Let me get to work, finalize this paperwork, and get back to focusing on tomorrow's party.

As I'm working on the tasks at hand, Ronnie yells out, "Boss Lady, you have a call on line 4."

Line 4 is a line only personal people have the number to, so it doesn't strike me as odd.

"Isis speaking."

"Isis, hey sorry to call you at work, but I just wanted you to know I'm well. I also wanted to send my regrets, but I won't be back until Saturday. Some unforeseen circumstances have come up and the meeting will be tomorrow instead of tonight. How are you doing?"

"The fuck, Avery, what do you mean? Nevermind that, did you go alone? I need contact information. Why are you calling me at the office instead of on my cell phone?"

"Yes, I'm good. Girl, I did call you from my other cell phone, but you didn't answer. So, I decided to call the office. I am safe and the west coast is so beautiful. I swear we gotta come back when you have time. It's just beautiful out here. His hospitality is impeccable and I assure you that everything is going just as planned with the exception of the meeting change. I'm texting you all the details now."

Taking a deep breath, it's almost like a sigh of relief that she's ok. Those cartel muthafuckas can be ruthless to say the least.

"Girl, I'm glad you're doing well and I've only been to the west coast one time. It would be nice to get back there again. Oh! let me fill you in on the tea of the day, I'll try to make a long story short. But, Lance came to the office today. He, Kupenda and Horisha got into a verbal shouting match. You should've seen that shit. He was begging Horisha to lay low on the money he owes her. But, they handled it well, I guess."

With both of us laughing she responded, "When I get back I'm giving her this money, so she can get the hell on. I can't believe this nigga, and here I am paying off one of his loose ends that really don't have shit to do with me. He keeps costing me money. I swear he gone pay me back with muthafucking interest. Well, I gotta go and you should have the information on your cell phone. I'll keep in touch with you, and please don't tell anyone where I am. I'll handle all that when I get back home."

"Your secret is safe with me. Stay dangerous, and please don't forget to wear your mask. We can't have you coming back with that COVID shit."

"No doubt. I'll talk to you later."

The call was disconnected.

What a relief, she's safe and sound. Her spirits seem to be up. I know she knows what she's doing. It just blows my mind that she's a woman in the game and no one actually suspects her at all. That's my girl. I think I'm about to call it a day. I've done enough and my mind is finally at rest with the Avery situation, so now I can go home and get everything in order for tomorrow. Throwing my hands in the air, I started doing my little cute girl dance while in my zone, here comes Ronnie.

"Boss Lady, you good? It looks like you having a seizure. Do you need some help?"

I just kept moving and gave him the finger.

I told him, "It's going down tomorrow! We got two purchase agreements today under Carrington & Associates, so I'm floating and ain't shit yo' hating ass can say to get me off this vibe. Now what do you need?"

"Damn, well, I just came in here to tell you Mr. Donahue was just rushed to the hospital. Someone caught him in the corner throwing up blood, so EMS was called and they came and picked him up."

With a serious facial expression, I asked him, "Are you fucking serious?"

"Um, yeah. While you were in here seizing, I was about to go flag them down. I thought they may have needed to take you too. But, for real, you gotta go see what's up. With all this going on, should I cancel the party for tomorrow?"

"As of right now, NO!. Deposits are already made and we won't get the money back. So, the show will go on."

"Well, I'm about to leave and go to the hospital. Did they say which one they took him to?"

"I believe they went to Karmanos Cancer Institute. Hurry up and go see what's up. I'll lock up and get Horisha and Kupenda together. Keep me posted please."

I grab my cell phone, purse, and keys. This shit is just happening way too fast. I was just in his office and he was reading me my rights. Now, only a few hours later, he's been rushed to the hospital. Fuck Cancer! I know this sounds selfish, but he gotta stick around to see me take over. That man has been so instrumental in my career, almost like a father. The only Caucasian man that never saw color when he looked at me. This can't be happening right now. Driving to the hospital, I sent text messages to my family to let them know I'll be late, and Kareem has to find a ride to the crib. Hell, he can call Ryan to pick him up.

As I'm riding down the expressway, I just had a few moments to talk with my ancestors. I asked them to look out for him, and not take him just yet. I know it's selfish, but I'm honest. I know it's inevitable but give him a little more time, if not for his family, do it for me. Before I knew it, I wiped my face. I couldn't believe tears were streaming down my face and I couldn't stop them. Was this the feeling I was feeling when I got up this morning when it just felt uncomfortable? But, I saw the bird, so I know everything is going to be ok. It just has to be. It can't go like this.

Arriving at the hospital, I was greeted by his wife and son. Immediately, my heart sank. But, what she said gave me a sense of so much peace within.

"Mrs. Donahue, how is he?"

"Isis, he's ok for right now. But, his time is drawing near, and I'm so glad to see you. You made it here before anyone else. I'll share this with you first and then, I'll ask that you leave and go be with your family. Get ready for tomorrow."

Awaiting her next sentence, she softly said, "He shared with me how he was leaving the company to you and he told me just a few minutes ago that if you think you're having that party without him tomorrow, then you're sadly mistaken. He said he's fighting this to the end, and the end ain't right now. On that note, we'll all be there to see him pass the torch to you tomorrow. Go get ready, and thanks for coming."

Before I could say anything, she embraced me. At that moment, I just knew everything was going to be ok.

"Thank you so much, Mrs. Donahue. I really appreciate your kind words and support, if you need anything please don't hesitate to call me."

"I will, Isis, thank you so much. Congratulations again, and we'll see you tomorrow."

Walking out the hospital, I felt that my call to the ancestors was heard and I am at peace with everything that's going on. It's all in divine order. It's about to go down. I just feel so relieved about the events of today. Now, it's time to go home and see what my crazy family has going on.

Thank you so much! I can't express my gratitude to the universe for everything thus far. All my craziness, the shit at work from De'Angelo, Lance, Kareem, Horisha, Kupenda, Ronnie, Avery, Dino, Ryan & Aniya, on to Strickland and Jaylen too. Everybody is connected in one way or another. I'm the common denominator and I've been kept this far. Thank you so much, ancestors and I'm glad to know y'all got my crazy ass.

Chapter 28

Isis

Finally pulling up to my house, it appears that Ryan and Aniya have made up because her car is outside. I wonder if Kareem is inside because I never heard anything from him about being picked up or catching a ride from his homies.

Entering the house, I just stood in the foyer and listened to the noise to attempt to figure out what was going on before I walked in. After removing my shoes and going to my room, I just sat on my bed and thought about the events of the day. Then, I noticed a Dolce & Gabbana bag hanging on my door. Should I open it or should I let it be a surprise? I mean it is in my house, but it ain't on my bed. It's just hanging there. Kareem probably put it in here thinking I was coming straight to the kitchen like I always do, then he could come and surprise me. Well, I'll just leave it like that and I won't ruin it. Let me go check on the children in the house. Hopefully, they were able to get that Strickland situation under control. Speaking of Strickland, I hope Avery is prepared for this bomb to drop. Maybe it's good she won't be here tomorrow, so she won't have to witness it first hand. But, shit with all the Facebook, TikTok, and Instagram, she won't miss it.

"Well, hey y'all, what's going on?"

All I could see was Ryan and Aniya at the table going over prom and graduation stuff.

I turn and ask them,"Where's Dino?"

"Here, I am mommy. I'm over here reading and working on my math homework."

"Ok, baby, well bring it to me when you finish, so I can check it."

"Mommy, that's ok. Last time, you checked it. I didn't get a good grade. Ryan said he'll help me with it."

The room erupted in laughter.

"Excuse me, little man, I know how to do math. Y'all just do it a different kind of way and that doesn't mean my way is wrong. Forget you, and Ryan ain't all that."

"Y'all good with the prom and graduation stuff?"

I asked as I nudged Ryan when I passed the table where the two of them were sitting.

"Yes, ma'am," Aniya answered, "My mom told me what the two of you all came up with and were getting everything together now. Thank you so much."

"Speaking of your mom, have you spoken to her?"

"I did this morning. She told me she had some stuff to handle, so she sent me money for dinner. You know my dad, well, he's straight I guess."

"That's good to hear. Y'all will be in attendance tomorrow, right?"

All in unison, they responded, "Yeah."

"Ryan, have you heard from Kareem?"

"Yeah, I talked to him earlier and he said he would be here after the studio session was over. He said he needed to finish up something that he was working on. But that's about it."

"Ok cool, what do y'all want for dinner?"

"Ma, you know we good and you on yo' own tonight. There's leftovers in the fridge from last night, so you can have at it."

I can't do anything, but shake my head. I swear they do too much. I guess leftovers it is.

Eating dinner and drinking wine, relaxing for the evening, I just actually wanted to take a quick shower before I get into the bed. Everything that happened today had me ready to turn my mind off. Before I could kiss my children goodnight, Kareem walks in. I proceeded to kiss the children and told them not to be up too late. I headed to my room.

"Hey, little one, I got a surprise for you. I'll be in there after I chop it up with the fam." I nodded my head and went to my room.

Doing a cute little strut, I knew I was right to follow my first mind and let that bag stay right where it was supposed to be. I know that man is super calculated. I think I know him.

Dancing and bobbing my head to the music in my mind, I got ready for my shower. Before I could turn around, he was standing here with the bag in his hand.

"I hope this fits. I picked it up the other day when we were at the mall. It's for tomorrow. I want you to look as amazing as you're gonna feel. Nothing tomorrow is going to interfere with what you got going on. You're a whole frequency and everybody's gonna try to be on your vibe. My baby did that. Congratulations, love."

"Thank you so much."

I kissed him and jumped in the shower. I washed the day off and proceeded to get out and grab my undergarments, so I could try the dress on. This man knows he has impeccable taste, especially when it comes to me. It fits perfectly and it's my favorite color, royal blue.

As I'm admiring it in the mirror, he hands me some shoes and says, "Pick a pair. I wasn't sure how you wanted to look, so I grabbed a few different pairs of shoes. Now, you can pick them yourself."

"Well, considering the pantsuit is royal blue, I'll go with the multicolored shoe. It's strappy and sexy, and my pedicured toes will look perfect in them."

We embraced and exchanged daily stories. Although, it was weird. It was oddly satisfying. After Kareem got out of the shower, he held me in his arms and he went to sleep.

Laying there listening to him breathe, I had to ask myself some tough questions. Can I really see him moving in with us? Do I like it the way it is? We've known each other for over 20 years. It's never been the right time for us to actually commit to one another, so I'm a little apprehensive. However, I do know I am in love with this man, and we have the bomb relationship. I just don't want it to change. But as long as we remain honest with one another, we can't go wrong. Before I started to drift off, I snuggled up in his arms and completed the night in his arms.

Chapter 29

The Celebration

Awakened by kisses, could this be just because of what today is? Is it something he's been wanting to do? Oh well, I can't overthink this shit. I'm just going to roll with the punches. Stretching and getting my body ready for the day, I'm unsure exactly how it's gonna go down, but I do know I don't feel that uncomfortable feeling like I did yesterday. Whatever it is, or however it goes, I'm coming out on top. I don't know any of the particulars for today's events because that is all on Ronnie, Kupenda, and Horisha. Hopefully, they come through for ya girl one time.

"Good morning, Gorgeous."

"Well, good morning to you too, Mary J. Blige."

Jokingly, we both laughed and hugged.

Kareem asked, "Are you ready for the big day? They are getting ready to pass the flag over to you. Can you handle the weight it's getting ready to bring?"

"Well, babe, you know what? I'm going to try my best to continue to be humble and not do too much. This is indeed a prestigious honor. Being the youngest agent of the company and being a sister of color, those facts alone are pressure. But, I've been raised by the best."

As I playfully hit him, I told him, "I think I know how to handle myself in heated situations."

"Well little one, today is all about you. Don't let no one or nothing make you feel you are not deserving of this elevation. You got this. What time do the festivities start?"

"I am going to guess and say noon. The office closes at 5, and typically no one is there after 5, considering what's going on, maybe they'll make an exception."

"Ok, well I'll grab the boys from school and we'll be there shortly after. We don't wanna miss any of the festivities."

"Thank you so much, I'll see you soon. Let me get myself together and get to the office."

"Well don't worry about the boys, I got them, and we'll see you later."

Doing my two step, I sashayed to the bathroom, took a quick shower and got dressed. I need to get out of here and get there early, so hopefully I can see what they got going on. I'm not going to pay any attention to no one inside this house until I get back home. Right now, I'm focusing on me and today.

As I'm getting myself together, I can't help but to get super excited, as I slip on this outfit. It fits like a glove. The pants fit so sexy because they make my booty look fierce. What really does it for me is the crossover top, it's to die for. I cannot forget these shoes. They are the shit. You can't tell me nothing. I'm out.

Today is moving kinda fast, but I promise to slow down and take it all in. I, honestly, don't know why I feel giddy. I have to admit I'm excited and nervous that the team has put this together on such short notice, or maybe it's the fact that Mr. Donahue has trusted me to lead the company and I really have some big shoes to fill. But as long as I'm rocking these stilettos, then I'm good. Can't no man up there rock these like me. Then, I had to laugh to myself and remember Ronnie is the truth in heels. I love my job.

Speaking of my job, the parking lot is pumped to be a little after 9am. But maybe those cars are the other people doing whatever it is they do, and normally I don't get here until almost 10 and half the lot is empty. Anywho, that has nothing to do with me. Sitting in the car attempting to mentally prepare myself for this fabulous day, I just say a prayer of gratitude to the ancestors and ask them to keep all the negativity away. When I get in here, I need to sign some paperwork and do a bit of finalization under

Keys Real Estate and get ready for the change over to Carrington & Associates.

"Surprise, girl, you made it here on time. Don't start nothing that you ain't gone keep up on Monday when you really gotta be here early."

Shocked that Ronnie and Kupenda are here super early.

With a smile on my face, I ask, "Why are the both of you here so early?"

Kupenda replies, "I wanted to do some more filing, but Ronnie told me to come help decorate before you got here. And when he saw you coming his extra self just yelled out, surprise!"

"That's typical Ronnie fashion. Kupenda, I really want you to know that you've jumped right in and although you've only been here less than a week, you've been amazing. Thank you so much."

"No, I want to thank you. I know all our run ins haven't been the best, but I'm glad you decided to give me a chance to stand on my own two feet. Now, I have the opportunity to do that. I don't gotta deal with bastards like Lance. So, *Thank You*!"

I acknowledged her gratitude with a nod and a wink, then went inside the office.

"Now, who sent roses to my job? And they're blue!"

Taking the card out of the card holder stand, it simply said, "Knock their socks off! Sincerely, Mrs. Donahue."

"Ronnie, be sure to send Mrs. Donahue a nice Edible Arrangement when this is over. She's been so gracious to me."

Ronnie says, "Got it down."

If the day continues like this, then I don't know if I'll be able to take much more. Let me take care of my legalities before the party starts, but hell sounds like it already has. So, you know what? One day of no work won't hurt. Nope, wrong thought process, sign the paperwork and be done. Actually, today is the last day that I'll sign anything under Keys Real Estate. Let me get to signing.

"Boss Lady, you got a delivery you need to sign for."

"Well, Ronnie, sign for it, so I can keep doing my work."

"Quit playing and get out here. You know you want us to see you in that pants suit that you think you look cute in."

Laughing to myself, I had to admit that he was right. Let me get out there, so I can get whatever this is.

Peeking out my door, I see two delivery guys, but I can't see any packages. Why are there two guys?

"Hi, I'm Isis. How can I help you?"

"Ms. Carrington, can you sign right here? We'll bring your package in."

I am still unsure as to who has sent me something. They leave out and bring back in these two huge boxes.

"Excuse me, sir, can you tell me who these are from?"

"Well, ma'am, the purchase order just says, Whitaker Construction."

"Oh, hell no! Take this shit back, right the fuck now. I don't want it. Return to the muthafucking sender."

As I am ranting, Ronnie says, "Boss Lady, what if it's from Avery? Don't start tripping just yet."

"Ok, Ronnie, you may be right."

Turning back to the delivery men, "Can you please place the boxes in my office?"

Pointing them in the correct direction and they proceeded to drop off the two boxes. What in the entire hell is in those boxes? I know I won't open it today, so it'll have to wait 'til Monday.

Just hanging around in Ronnie's office, Horisha walks in.

"Good morning to the top sales associate of Carrington & Associates, how are you today?"

Shocked, she replied, "Top sales associate? Don't you have the other agents here?"

"Indeed, there are other associates, but right now, I'm talking to you. Do you want to know how much commission you'll get off those two houses yesterday?"

"You already crunched the numbers?"

"Of course, I did. I don't play about my money."

Leaning over to grab a post-it note from Ronnie's desk, I wrote down what she'll be getting and passed it to her. When she looked at the paper, she let out the biggest yet muffled scream possible.

"Oh my goodness, this is all mine? Don't you get a cut too?"

I do, but I already subtracted my portion. This is all yours, and the minute they close is when you get paid."

"How long before closing?"

"Well, we're looking at about another 6 weeks. It depends on if they pass all the inspections and the loan goes through, but I don't see any of that posing any problem. Just imagine how many more you'll do before the six weeks are up. Keep up the good work."

Smiling and almost in tears, she responded, "Yes, ma'am, I will. I also have to remember to use my ABCs.

Time must be flying by because before I knew it, the entire office was filled with guests. The caterers had shown up and everything was in place. Kareem, the boys, and Aniya were all here. Horisha's family–Strickland and her mother– as well as Kupenda's mother had joined us as well. I would like to think that this is a grand event, even Ronnie's parents came out to join us. What could possibly go wrong? The other colleagues came down, even Mr. and Mrs. Donahue and their children were in attendance.

I grabbed the mic and began to speak.

"First of all, I'd like to thank everyone for coming out to share in this grand experience with me. It is indeed an honor to be standing before you today as a young, black woman that will now lead this company. Mr. Donahue, I owe everything to you. Thank you for believing in me and giving me a chance fresh out of school. I honor you today. I won't get all teary eyed and become a cry baby, but I want to let everyone know that you all mean the world to me and nothing would be possible without the help from my personal team, Ronnie, Horisha, and Kupenda. Of course, I also appreciate the rest of my colleagues here at the firm that have contributed to the success of this agency. I'm looking forward to continuing the legacy of Mr. Donahue and starting my own. Now, the floor and the mic are open, turn up the music, and everyone eat up. Enjoy.

As I was mingling and working the crowd, it was such a feeling of extreme gratitude that came over me and I had to take a moment. I had to leave the room just to gather my feelings. I didn't want to run my make-up and have everyone see me as a crybaby.

Before long, I heard this voice come across the mic, it was that of my son, Ryan.

"Mom, where are you? Come up here, I want to say a few words."

As he’s speaking, I can't do anything, but cry because he just has a way with words. I’m standing there letting everyone see me cry and I just said I didn’t want this to happen. When he finished, he passed the mic to Kareem.

In true Kareem fashion, he began to speak.

“I knew it was something about you when I met you 20 plus years ago. I’ve watched you grow and develop into the woman I see standing in front of me today. I’ve learned so much from you, and I don’t tell you often, but today I want to profess my feelings for you. I want to let you know how much I adore and care about you. Talking about surprises, Kareem ques the music. It started playing and he performed a song that he had written just for me. Still crying hard as a baby, Ryan grabbed me a chair and sat me down, so I could see the performance.

Overjoyed, I honestly can’t hear all he’s saying, but I do know I’m crying like a big baby. I mean the ugly cry. You know the kind that Viola Davis does in any movie she stars in. Before I knew it, the music stopped playing. As I was wiping my face, he was looking me right in my eye, which meant he was on one knee with a ring.

“Well, are you going to be my forever lady or what?”

I swear I can't hear too much of anything because the office just erupted in a bunch of screams and claps.

"Yes!"

I stood up and he placed a beautiful 3-carat oval cut diamond with so many other diamonds around it. I just stood there in total shock. I looked over at Ryan and he was standing there with his phone recording every minute of it. Aniya and Dino also had their phones up. The next voice I then heard was that of Mr. Donahue.

He then said, "Well, I guess this has now become an engagement party, but not until I officially pass the keys to you. You've done well and I'm excited to pass the torch. Make me proud."

Grabbing the keys, I gave him one of the biggest hugs and told him I wouldn't let him down.

Taking all that in, looking at the rock on my hand, all those questions I had last night were out the window, I love this man and this man loves me. The party was going great. I didn't think anything could go wrong.

I was so wrong. As I surveyed the room, I saw Lance. He was standing in the back. He had his drink and I'm not even sure if he spoke to Aniya, but he was standing out like a sore thumb. I decided not to acknowledge him and I kept enjoying the festivities. Now, was he here to see if I got the package? Did Avery send it because she wasn't able to make it? There's only one way to find out. Let me go ask.

Making my way through the crowd, I noticed that he was staring at Strickland with an uneasy look. Every now and then, he would look at Strickland, then Horisha, and then he'd look at Aniya. And if I know those looks, I swear he is getting ready to blow the shit up because I know Horisha hasn't mentioned that to him, as of yet. But he has to keep his cool because he doesn't want Aniya to become alarmed.

Walking up to him, I say, "Hey, Mr. Whitaker. Are you ok? You seem to be a bit off from your usual self. Is everything ok?"

"Yeah. I just came to see if Avery was here because she didn't come home last night. I know I make some fucked up mistakes, but she's never not come home."

"Well maybe she just needs a few days, she's fine. I'm sure. Speaking of Avery, do you happen to know who sent the two large boxes from Whitaker Construction?"

"Yeah, that was from the three of us. We wanted to let you know we are happy for you. If you'll excuse me, then I'll be right back."

Now, I know shit is about to hit the fan. He ain't never brushed me off like that. I gotta do some damage control and I mean like right now. I didn't get over to Horisha fast enough because he walked up behind her and whispered something in her ear. Whatever he said, it caused her to jump and spill her drink. Before I could get over there to them, she yells for security to come escort him out the building.

With her yelling for security, her voice alarmed Strickland, so he walked over there to check on her. As he approached her, Lance looked as if he saw a ghost. More like he saw himself 20 years ago, there they stood looking eye to eye. There was only one way out of the problem. It was time for Horisha to tell Lance the truth. Stickland looked at his mother and asked, "Are you alright, Ma?"

Lance looked and said, "Ma? What do you mean, ma?"

Strickland looked at him square in the eyes and said, "Look, old time, I don't know who you are, but you are standing a bit too close to my momma and I don't like the vibe you are giving off. I'm gone need you to step back a few feet. Shit, it's COVID out here. Back up and give her 6 feet."

"What do you mean old time? Young blood, you gone respect yo' elders. You don't know me like that. Me and this woman go way back."

So now, the two are exchanging words. I had to do a quick survey of the room and as luck would have it Mr. and Mrs. Donahue and a few of the other colleagues had left the celebration. But Kareem, Ryan, and Aniya were headed this way. I swear the tension in this room is so damn thick that you can cut it with a knife.

Aniya walks up and says, "Dad, what is going on? How do you know this lady? What do you mean yall go way back?"

"Baby, I've known this woman from before I met your mother, and I just need to talk to her for a few minutes."

As Strickland chimed in, "Now, ain't the place for you to be talking to her. You can get at her outside these walls. She is at work."

Before Lance could respond, Horisha said, Strickland, don't disrespect your father. Lance meet Strickland, your son. Strickland meet Lance, your father.

It was so quiet you could've heard a rat piss on cotton. The look on everybody's faces was something out of a movie. Aniya surveyed what just took place and she started crying and took off running. Ryan ran after her to check on her, and the three of them Horisha, Strickland, and Lance just stood there in total shock.

Then, when I think things couldn't get any worse, Dino runs up to me and says, "Mommy, look at the phone I'm on Facebook Live and it says 1500 viewers."

Stunned to say the least, I just asked him, "Baby, how long have you been live on Facebook?"

"Um, ever since you took the stage to thank everyone for coming."

I just shook my head and said, "Pass me the phone. Let's cut this short."

As I was ending the live stream, I was hoping to myself that he didn't have a good view of things, but hell I can't be sure at this point. Not long after I ended the live, my phone rang, and of course, it was Avery.

I took a deep breath and said, "Let the damn drama begin."

About the Author

KeanaMonique is a Michigan native that is usually found performing manicuring services for clients at her home-based nail salon called *N'Chanted Nails*. She enjoys spending time with her family and traveling. Becoming a published author had never been on her bucket list, but the moment she became one, the possibilities became endless. She has written and published six books titled: *Pieces of Me Volumes 1 & 2, 365 Days of Life, Love & Pain: Adding to the Puzzle, THOT Chronicles: The Tale of Isis Carrington. THOT Chronicles 2: Isis Seeks Vengeance.* And now *Thot Chronicles 3: Isis' Final Reign*, to complete the trilogy. To contact her you can send an email to:

Keanamonqiue@freebirdexpressions.com.
www.facebook.com/freebirdexpressions,
www.instagram.com/freebirdexpressions,
www.freebirdexpressions.com

CPSIA information can be obtained
at www.ICGtesting.com
Printed in the USA
JSHW020747290722
28478JS00002B/100